WINNING HER HEART

EMILY HAYES

1

"**Y**ou better start catching up, or I'm going to fall asleep," I shouted across the court to Tiffany and flashed a cheeky smile.

"Keep on laughing, but it's not every day that a flight attendant makes a tennis pro sweat at tennis. This is definitely a win for me any way you look at it," Tiffany responded, a determined look on her face. She was not taking her loss lightly. She was the kind of woman who brought her A-game to everything she did, and the current game was no exception. She knew she wasn't winning, but she definitely enjoyed seeing me break a sweat, running around the court trying to save the ball.

"There is no way you are beating me at this game, you'll have to be better than this to win the US Open in a few weeks." she shouted from the end of the court before serving. The ball flew past my shoulder, nearly hitting me. "Sorry!" she apologized, a meek expression on her face.

"Ouch! You are even worse at this than I thought," I said. I chuckled, rubbing my shoulder from the imaginary impact.

"Douchebag!" She shouted as she prepared to serve the next set.

I was definitely going to let her win this one. She whacked the ball and landed near the baseline. I ran to receive the ball but stopped mid-track when a sharp pain shot down through my left knee. "Ouch!" I cussed loudly, bending over. Tiffany dropped her racket and came running. By the time she made it to where I was, I had already sat down and started massaging my knee.

"What just happened?" she inquired, the worry barely concealed in her large blue eyes.

"I think it was just a cramp," I replied, shrugging it off.

"Are you sure, Sloane? It looked like it was painful," she said as she knelt onto the ground next to me.

"Yeah. Just a cramp," I replied. "Don't tell your dad about this, he'll get all worked up for nothing, and I don't need him all over me before the Open," I added, trying to get up. Dan Jacobs, my coach, also happened to be my best friend Tiffany's dad. She and I had been best friends from kindergarten. Dan, a former world champion, always wanted her to follow in his footsteps and go pro, but Tiffany had neither the desire nor the self-discipline it took to be a professional athlete. That's why Dan was delighted when I took an interest in the sport. The entirety of my childhood weekends were spent with Dan and Tiffany at the tennis court.

She looked at me skeptically, obviously concerned about my decision to keep this from him. "My lips are sealed. I have nothing to tell him. Well, other than the fact that I lost four sets to you. In fact, I won't even say that," Tiffany teased, trying to lighten the mood.

"I don't know about you, but I am beat. Maybe we've had enough for today. How about we go somewhere and have something to drink?"

"I think I could use a nice cold pineapple juice right about now," Tiffany said as she wiped the sweat trickling down the side of her face, landing on her chest with a towel.

"I was thinking more along the lines of pina coladas, but the pineapple juice sounds like a compromise I can live with," I replied while packing my racket into its bag. I was exhausted, and the afternoon heat was not making it any better.

I lazily dragged my racket on the ground as Tiffany and I strolled to the locker room. My arms and legs were burning from the intense workout. Thankfully, the locker room was empty. I wasn't in the mood to deal with many people. I keyed in the passcode to the lock on my steel locker, grabbing my favorite grey towel and shower gel; I shuffled to the showers. There's nothing as refreshing as a cold shower after an intense workout, is there? The cold water droplets from the shower-head rolled over my body, cooling every inch and releasing the tension from my tight and exhausted muscles. After the shower, I changed into my mustard yellow romper and a pair of stylish white sandals. I looked into the mirror to find a set of big brown eyes looking back at me. My hair was frizzy from the sweat and humidity. I could try to fix it, but what was the point? I heard a throat clear behind me and turned around to find Tiffany looking stunning in her baby blue sundress and coal-black sun-hat. "Shall we go now, or do you want to keep watching yourself age in that mirror?"

I chuckled lightly at the comment. "Shut up." Tiffany was a tease, but that's one of the things that made her so fun to be around.

We strolled two blocks down to a slightly busy street and turned the corner into one of the city's best-kept secrets, Marie's Juice Bar. The place had brightly colored walls, and soft music emanated from hidden speakers, creating the illusion that it came from the walls themselves. The ambiance was welcoming and relaxed, and that was precisely what we both needed. We got a table outside by the window, giving us a view of the people walking by outside. A young man walked towards us smiling. "Welcome to Marie's Juice Bar," he said, handing us menus. "My name is Fredrick. What would you like to have this lovely afternoon?"

Tiffany gently placed the menu on the wooden table, looked up at Fredrick, and with a smile on her face, said, "I think a glass of pineapple juice will do, go heavy on the ice." I was still scanning the menu, undecided on what to order, when Fredrick started fidgeting, seemingly impatient with my indecisiveness. "I think I'll have the same," I said, raising my eyes to meet the flat look on his face. He flashed a fake smile, took the menus, and left.

We settled back into our seats and sat in silence for a bit before Tiffany leaned back over the table, eyes staring directly at me. "So, Sloane, without beating around the bush, if the US Open goes as expected you should have an easy road to the final. It is most likely you will meet Jane Parker in the final and we all know she has been on FIRE lately. If you hadn't lost to Michaels in the last tournament, do you think you would have beaten Parker in the final?"

I sighed heavily; I had been dreading the question all day. "I'm okay, just a little nervous- Parker really is playing well and it has been so long since I was drawn against her actually. I know you've seen the head-lines, 'Has Age Finally Caught Up with Sloane Smith?' Or my favorite one yet, 'Smith's Future Suddenly in Question over Michaels Loss.' They honestly need to back off and just let me play. I'm 100% focussed on the US Open. The draw suits me. I am confident I will make the final. I know I can win another Grand Slam. I'm still Sloane Smith you know. I'm still the same Sloane Smith, the champion, with all those Grand Slam wins under my belt. I might be get-ting older but I'm not dead yet." I rolled my eyes, unable to hide the disdain I had for all those clickbait publications.

"They can go to hell; you clearly still have years of playing left in you. Judging from your performance today, you're in good shape. Well, I'm no Jane Parker, but you beat me four sets in a row without even breaking a sweat." Tiffany spoke with the reassuring voice that always made me feel like we were family.

I was about to speak when Fredrick brought out our drinks in beautiful long glasses with black and white striped straws on a black ceramic tray. Placing our drinks on the table, "Enjoy your drinks," he said, then disappeared through the line forming at the entrance.

We sat in silence for a while, sipping our drinks as we scrutinized the people around us, from the people seated inside to those walking by on the sidewalk. I was busy watching a man pass by in a very un-flattering jacket for the weather when a nearly inaudible whisper from Tiffany brought me back to my senses.

"Cute guy, three o'clock." She nudged me while gesturing towards one of the waiters at the far end of the restaurant. I turned quickly, trying to catch a glimpse, but he had already disappeared into the back.

Tiffany smiled at my failed attempt. "Not so subtle, are we, Sloane?"

"Here he comes," she said, following his every move with just her eyes.

I sat up straight in my chair, trying to have a good look at this guy. He was a tall, handsome man wearing a buttoned-down shirt that was tucked a bit too tightly into his beige shorts with an apron tied snuggly around his waist. He had a tapered haircut and round black-framed glasses and was exactly Tiffany's type. We watched as he laid the customer's orders on the table, inaudibly said some words, then smiled beautifully, exposing a perfect set of pearly white teeth.

"Damn! That's one handsome man," Tiffany exclaimed, still following him with her eyes.

"Calm down before you melt all the ice left in your glass," I teased.

"I am calm. I just simply appreciate beauty at its finest. I am totally going to get his number before we get out of here. God knows it's been really dry down there for the last couple of months," Tiffany said as a cheeky grin spread across her face.

"Ugh, that's way too much information than I want to have about your terrible sex life in this juice bar right now," I exclaimed with false indignation.

Tiffany rolled her at me. "Oh, you're one to talk. At least I have a love life. You're telling me to calm down when the only action you're getting is from your purple battery operated friend in the cabinet beside your bed. Maybe it's time you joined me and started living a little."

"Ouch! Now that's just mean. Plus, I'm too busy with practice and tournaments. Maybe when the season is over, I'll go on a couple of dates and see how it pans out."

"Both you and I know that is just an excuse, Sloane. You haven't been yourself or even dated anyone after the whole thing with Celine."

"It is not an excuse. I'm totally over Celine. I just don't have time or mental capacity for anyone or really anything besides tennis right now," I sighed and leaned back into my chair, wishing we could talk about literally anything else.

"Can I at least hook you up with my friend, Jen? She's super hot, plus she's exactly your type."

"No, and please don't talk about my

type in public," I responded without giving her a single second more to think of the idea. "Well, that was a little too fast," Tiffany said, eyebrow raised.

"I just don't want to see anyone; let it go. Also, keep your voice down. I don't want the whole world in my business. You know my sexuality is 100% NOT public knowledge," I whispered.

"You can't hide in the shadows forever, Sloane, but *fine*. You win today, but that's only because I have bigger fish to fry. Now watch and learn," she replied, a heavy hint of resignation in her voice before getting up and heading straight for the handsome waiter, who was now standing alone by the counter. She walked up to him, smiling and flirting; one would have thought they had known each other for years with how close she was standing to him. I watched as she handed him what I could only assume was her business card before she sauntered back to our table.

Tiffany wiggled her eyebrows, a triumphant look on her face. "Guess who has a date for this weekend? Take notes, Sloane Smith, *that's* how it's done."

I rolled my eyes so far back into my head I thought they would fall in and took the final sip of my drink. After finishing up, we paid the bill and got up to leave with a hawk-eyed Tiffany nearly tripping over herself in search of her hot new crush.

2

"You've got this, Sloane. Remember: keep the swing firm, slice the ball, and watch out for blind spots. You're going to need a lot more than that if you want to beat her," Dan's voice was in my head. He was right; this was the final of the US Open- as predicted by myself, Tiffany and the world's sports media it was myself and Jane Parker in the final. The media were backing Parker to take the championship. She had dispatched her Semi Final opponent as though she was nothing, whereas I had let my Semi Final drag out to 3 sets and then I had let the third set become a scrap. But, nevertheless, a win is a win. This was the Final of the US Open and I would be damned if I was going to let it slip out of my grasp and into hers.

"*US Open final! Jane Parker against Sloane Smith,*" the announcer's voice boomed over the crowd as I walked over and took my position on the court. I took a deep breath, inhaling the crisp New York air, trying my best to tap into the audience's energy. There really isn't anywhere else like Flushing Meadows in New York, is there? I have always loved to play there. It's the US Open, one of the top competitions in the world. It is America. It is Home. My life as a tennis pro is all hotels and travelling, but as a proud American, the US Open is the tournament that is home for me.

You could feel the excitement of the stands right from the center of the court. "*Server, Sloane Smith,*" he continued. My eyes swept across the stands before finally landing on my entourage; Dan flashed me a comforting smile that definitely helped with the nerves.

The crowd fell silent.

One of the ball girls handed me a tennis ball. I held on to it, squeezing it, before nervously bouncing it a few times on the ground to release tension. In one swift move, I grasped it, feeling the rough felt cover, before I threw it up into the air and whacked it across the court, kicking off the match. Parker rushed to return fire, setting off a tense set of back and forth strokes between us before missing a swing and landing me my first point *"Fifteen- Love,"* the announcer pronounced, his voice echoing through the mostly silent arena.

Parker's first serve was out. She was obviously nervous; the realization spurred a boost of confidence; what I was doing was clearly working. Ultimately, I was the great Sloane Smith, she might be playing like nobody could beat her, but she was still young and clearly intimidated to see a champion across the net. Her second serve was successful, and elicited a backhand response from me, causing what felt like a surge of electricity to course through my veins. I was pumped; this game was mine. After almost two minutes of back-to-back shots, Parker whacked the ball, sending it flying to the opposite end of the court. I managed to receive it and land a similar move. Amped up, Parker fired back and sent the ball straight through to the far left end of the court, startling me, and in my attempt to change direction, I felt a sharp pain course through my left knee. I placed my racket on the ground and tried shaking off the pain by doing a short walk to the opposite side of the court and back. With each step, the pain got sharper. *This can't be happening to me. Not now. This is my chance. I have to win.* Ignoring the pain, I paced up and down the court before getting back to where I dropped my racket and stood ready to receive Jane's serve. *One more point. Just one more point. That's all I need.* Jane served the ball from behind the baseline, sending it towards the center of my side of the court. I darted into action to receive it and had barely moved three steps when I felt an even more excruciating pain that sent me spiraling to the ground screaming in pain. I mumbled to myself as the medical crew rushed towards me. I rolled over onto my side, the pain now unbearable.

I knew there and then that the US Open dream was over for me.

THE SUBTLE HINT of antiseptic that hovered over the hospital corridors immediately struck my nose as I was wheeled into the emergency room. My medical support team had insisted on a scan straight away. The bright white fluorescent light bulbs and beeping machines provided even more stimulation to my already over-stimulated mind. It took me a minute to recognize the beautiful middle-aged doctor who walked in. "Hey, Sloane. Tough game, huh?" It was Dr. Amira Alvarez, the best sports physician in New York (and quite probably the whole of the US). She took a hard look at me before noticing just how petrified I was. "It's just a bump on the road. We are all here for you. You're going to be fine, don't worry about a thing. Let's get the tests done and see just how big this bump is." On her instruction, I did my best to sit up straight while she observed and performed a series of examinations on my leg and then proceeded to write furiously on the little notepad beside my bed. She then looked up towards me. "One last thing. You're going to need an x-ray, just to rule out the possibility of a fracture and an MRI to see just exactly what we are looking at. Right, lets get this ice pack back on your knee." I nodded, my heart now in my throat. It had to be my ligaments, a fracture too- surely not? I could lose months, or an entire season. *This can't be happening to me. Not at this point in my career. Not at my age.*

"In the meantime, I'm going to give you these for the pain." She handed me a cocktail of differently colored pills and a glass of water. "Disclaimer, they're going to make you really sleepy." I nodded as I downed the handful of tablets with a tall glass of water. Dr. Alvarez walked out before coming back with a nurse in tow, "Now Nurse Jackie is going to put you on the wheelchair and take you for the other tests. "Hi, Nurse Jackie," I barely managed as the slurring from the medication began to kick in. I did my best to help as she lifted me from the bed and onto the wheelchair by the side of my bed before getting knocked out cold.

I TRIED to open my eyes and found my face bathed in a blinding flash of light. *Am I dead? Is this heaven? Hell?* The thought frightened me, causing me to stir and wake my dad, who was seated in the bedside chair, head on the bed, right next to me. He rubbed his eyes and looked up to see me struggling with the amount of light on my face. He promptly got up to adjust the blinds, which had been allowing the bright halo of light to wash over my face from the top of the window. "You're awake." I nodded sleepily, still trying to get my bearings. "How are you feeling?" he asked as he sat back down.

"Better, I guess, but—" Before I could finish my statement, he shot up again from his seat. "Let me go get the doctor. Those drugs really knocked you out. We've been waiting for you to get up for a couple of hours now."

My heart rate quickened as he briskly

walked out of the room and, within a few minutes, returned with Dr. Álvarez in tow. The doctor began to check my vitals as my dad sat back in his seat. "How are you feeling?"

"Give it to me straight, Doc, how bad is it? I blurted out, unable to maintain the wait any longer.

Dr. Alvarez smiled. "Straight to the point, as usual, I see." She took her notepad out of her pocket and had a look, her eyebrows furrowed from the seriousness of the situation before turning her attention back to me. "Well, the good news is there are no fractures and no permanent damage to the structure of the leg, so you will be able to play tennis again eventually."

I sighed as a wave of relief flooded my body. *Not all is lost.* I squeezed my dad's hand and gave myself a couple of minutes to take it all in before turning my attention back to the doctor. "Okay, and what's the bad news?" The doctor scratched her forehead, absent-mindedly wiping the sweat that had formed on her brow. "You've ruptured a knee ligament- your anterior cruciate ligament. You'll need a surgery to repair things in there. Then extensive physical therapy and time." I avoided her gaze as she paused to look at me before continuing, "I'm estimating 6 months absolute best case scenario but much more likely it will be a year."

"Are you serious? Being off the court so long could completely ruin my career. I can't afford that right now. I have too much to lose! Age isn't on my side" I was unable to conceal the shock and anguish in my voice.

The doctor took a step back before sighing deeply, "Anything sooner than that, and it will happen again."

I sat back in my hospital bed, trying to take in the shocking implications of the doctor's words. My mind went white, completely unable to comprehend any information as the doctor politely excused herself and left me and my dad in the room. It wasn't long before a flood of tears welled up in my eyes, and the knowledge of the harsh reality took a firm hold in the pit of my stomach as those tears fell in big sobs of grief, unleashing the stabbing pain in my chest out into the otherwise eerily silent hospital room. I didn't know how, but I was going to get through this. Tennis was my entire life, and I was going to be a Grand Slam champion once again, even if it killed me.

3

I squinted, narrowing my eyes to try and decipher what time it was on the clock on my bedside table. It had been hours since I woke up, but I hadn't gotten out of bed, not to mention had a single bite to eat. I wasn't really hungry, but that was beside the point. I had promised my dad and Coach Dan that I would try, and so I would. I dragged myself from the bed, strapping my left leg into a full length brace that stopped any movement from my knee, took hold of my crutches and wedged them under my arms and began my journey from my room to the kitchen. I moved slowly through the spacious corridor filled on either side with a mix of framed pictures of my family, mixed in with my medals and trophies. I couldn't help the feeling that the awards, and the trophies served as a painfully cruel reminder of my past glory. I had had injuries before of course. Any professional sports person has- they are a hazard of the job. But this one had potential to keep me from playing for up to a year and I didn't have that kind of time. I wasn't getting any younger. I used to be a champion, but that was a power I could no longer embody. I took a deep breath and swallowed hard; I wasn't going to let this get the better of me.

I moved past the corridor and into the living room. The bright light from the large living room windows startled me, causing me to rub my eyes in a mixture of confusion and discomfort. On the left side was a large lounging area with white leather seats on a dark grey feathery carpet and an elegant glass table that stood proudly in the middle of the room. A large television hung on the wall. I had this beautiful expensive house that on an average year I spent very little time in because I was always travelling to the next tournament and living out of hotels. Now I was spending plenty time at home and I wish I could say I was enjoying it.

I continued moving to the far right, towards the open plan kitchen where I knew Jessica had prepared something for me to eat, just in case I came out. I picked up a carefully sealed plate from the marble countertop at the center of the kitchen. I headed towards the terrace, where I made myself comfortable at the crafted wooden table and squeezed in between the four chairs that rested facing the garden. I unwrapped the cling film to find the standard breakfast—some oats, a slice of toast, a couple of hardboiled eggs and half an avocado, and a couple of slices of mango.

"You know, if you just asked for some help, you wouldn't have to eat soggy oats or choke on your cold toast." Startled, I turned around to find my father walking towards me. "I like my oats this way. Plus, a little choking now and again produces character, if you ask me," I responded as light-heartedly as possible before taking a large spoonful of oats.

He walked up to the table and pulled the seat right next to me. "I see someone is in a better mood than usual."

I nodded slowly and said, "Must be the sunshine. I heard it works wonders."

"Then I'm sure your mind will be blown away when you find out it's out here every single day."

I rolled my eyes, unable to hide my smile; I had to give it to him; he always knew how to make me smile.

He leaned back into his chair, a tender look on his face. "I know how bad you want to compete. But you'll get them next time."

"Mmph," I grunted simply, trying my best to hide the sting of my situation. "It was stupid of me to keep pushing myself so hard. I did know, well, beforehand that my knee wasn't 100%, but I carried on anyway."

Concerned, he stretched his hand and put it over mine. "Hey, don't say that. It wasn't stupid. You're a champ; sometimes, these things happen. Plus, what kind of champion would you be without a little adversity now and again?"

I looked up at him and smiled. "Grand

Slam trophy or not, at least I always have you."

"Of course you do, honey. Now finish your breakfast and go take a shower. You stink. Plus, the doctor will be here any minute now."

I sniffed myself, suddenly feeling very self-conscious. It had been a few days since my last shower. There was a special shower stool and handrail; the shower had been altered to accommodate my new requirements. "Doctor?" I asked, unable to hide my confusion.

"Did you forget? Dr. Alvarez is coming over."

I continued to stare at him. This all sounded like brand new information.

"You know she said she would visit and check up on you."

Before I could respond, we heard a ring on the doorbell. "Too late. I guess that's her. What's a little stink in the grand scheme of things anyway?" It was only a few moments before Jessica, my housekeeper and all around personal assistant, walked onto the terrace, followed closely by Dr. Alvarez.

"Hello Sloane, Mr. Smith. I hope you

have been well," Doctor Alvarez said smiling at us. Her lipstick was dark red and she looked just as striking as usual.

"I've been alright, considering the circumstances. I'm just tired of lugging this thing with me everywhere I go," I said, pointing at the brace on my leg.

"I'm going to have a good look at your leg but all being well we can reduce the time spent in the brace gradually and look at gradually re-introducing weight bearing. Of course, you will still have to use crutches for a while, but I'm sure it'll be an improvement."

I smiled as relief swept over my body; it was finally looking like there is some light at the end of the tunnel. This nightmare was going to be over soon.

"Shall we go inside?" the doctor asked as she gestured towards the huge glass doors.

I followed my dad and Dr. Alvarez into the living room. She immediately placed my leg on a tiny wooden stool for support and removed the brace having a good look at the knee and assessing movement.

The scar on my knee looked foreign to

me still as I was so used to seeing my leg in the brace now.

Dr. Alvarez noted something in her notepad. "Okay, let's try and put a little weight through it.

My dad got up and walked towards me before extending his hand. Instinctively I took it and began to stand up. First putting all my weight on my right, non-injured leg before gradually gaining confidence and allowing myself to put a little weight through my left."

"It feels a little tingly," I said, my eyebrow raised in worry.

"That's perfectly normal. It has to get used to being stood on again after not being in use for such a long time."

"See, I told you that you're going to be fine. You've always been a champion, a fighter," my dad said while patting me on the back.

Dr. Alvarez smiled. It seemed like a good sign. "Does it hurt anywhere, especially your knee?"

I turned my attention back to her and shook my head; this was going better than I expected.

"Okay, now, lets do a few steps supported by your father. I want no more than 50% of your weight through it."

Placing my arm over my dad's shoulder, I began to walk, one small step at a time. I was doing it! I was actually doing it! 50% maybe, but it was a start.

"OK enough, have a sit down. You will need to get used to it again. With a little professional help, you will be perfectly alright and back on the court in no time." She spoke without looking up at me, furiously writing something in her notepad.

"So what's next, Doc?" my dad asked in a flat tone that said the doctor wasn't doing him any favors in his attempt to sound confident.

"Well, the leg looks good post surgery, there isn't any pain, and she has a good range of movement. We need to gradually work to increase time out of the brace and supported weight bearing. I am having a set of bars delivered to you that will act as handrails to support you as you begin walking again." The doctor paused to let the news sink in; my heart sank. I knew I wouldn't be able to play for a while but hearing the words from the doctor's mouth made it feel so much more real. She noted the fallen expression on my face and cleared her throat before continuing, "Don't worry, you are making a great recovery, and everything is progressing perfectly. You will be able to play again. But to make a full recovery, one good enough to be able to play tennis at a competitive level, you will need a physical therapist continuing to work with you every day. I believe your current therapist has had to leave urgently to take care of her sick mother?" She shifted in her seat and began searching for something in the pockets of her white coat. She fished out several business cards and handed them to me.

"On request from your coach and your dad, I took time to look around for the perfect physical therapist for you. Those are the ones I would recommend."

I shuffled through the small deck of business cards reading through the names and qualifications. "Okay, Doc, they all look impressive, but who would you specifically recommend. Have you worked with any of these people before?"

Dr. Alvarez extended her hand, and I handed the cards back to her. She narrowed her eyes behind her glasses as she started to shuffle through them until she stopped and pulled out a particular card and scanned it with her eyes before handing it back to me. I looked at it. It read simply, *Brooke Miller* and a phone number.

"Brooke is an old colleague and a personal friend of mine. She's practiced for about 12 years, and we have worked together on a number of cases. I think she is exceptionally good at what she does. I also think you might get on well with her. Which will help because you will need to spend a lot of time with her. I also know she is currently available and also local."

"She sounds great, I'll set up a meeting, and we can get started as soon as possible," my dad chimed in.

Dr. Alvarez looked at her watch. "It seems like my time here is done. I have a couple of more house calls to make. It seems like it's injury season all of a sudden."

"One last thing, Sloane, don't rush things. A slight pain is normal, anything more speak to Brooke or call me directly. Don't put too much pressure on yourself. Okay?"

I could not help but smile as I nodded. "Thanks, Doc."

"Alright. I'll see you again in a couple of days."

My dad followed behind Dr. Alvarez as he escorted her to the door. A wave of what felt like a mixture of relief and anxiety washed over me. It was finally time to work on getting my life back together, and that was just as scary as it was exciting. I held on tightly to the business card that was now in my hands, opened my palm, and began to study it; the material was sturdy and the font a beautiful wavy blue. For some reason, it inspired confidence. Little did I know that the woman it belonged to would inspire that and so much more.

4

SLOANE

I slouched myself even deeper into my living room couch and took another sip of the iced coffee on the nearby table. *Damn, that's good,* I thought to myself as I continued to devour the pages of Geoffrey Scott's *The Little Notes*. The one good thing about this whole thing was that it had provided me with so much free time. Time I previously didn't have to catch up on all the other things I loved doing. I was taken, engulfed, in the romantic fantasy, when the ring of the doorbell startled me, pulling me back into my reality. *This is why real-life sucks. Why can't it be a cheesy Romcom where everything goes great and ends with everyone living happily ever after?* I sighed and gripped my crutches, hoisting myself up from the chair before slowly walking over to the door. Semi weight bearing was getting more fun, I thought to myself. I wondered who it could be. Jessica was already gone for the day, and neither Coach Dan nor Tiffany had said they are coming over. My dad had gone back to his house to get some repairs done, so I was at a loss. I took a deep breath and opened the door to find the most gorgeous woman I had ever seen standing casually by the door. I stood still, my eyes fixated on her, completely tongue-tied. She smiled, momentarily exposing a gorgeous set of pearly white teeth. Her blue Adidas sweatsuit clung to her slightly muscular body perfectly, almost as if it had been made especially for her. As she shifted the white duffel bag she was carrying to her other shoulder, singular wisps of her short dark hair fell onto her face. My heart rate suddenly quickening, I gripped the cold steel handle of the door, sliding it open.

"Hey, you must be Sloane Smith. I'm Brooke, Brooke Miller, your new physiotherapist." She ran her fingers through her hair, removing it from her face as she spoke and exposing sparkling blue eyes that shone as she smiled. Her voice was low and husky and even sexier than I had anticipated.

"Nice to meet you, Brooke," I said as I extended my hand for a handshake. Her grip was just as I expected—strong and firm. She cleared her throat, drawing my attention to the fact that I was still clutching her hand. My face flushed from the embarrassment as I quickly let go. *So much for a first impression, Sloane.*

"Come on in." I stood to the side and gestured towards the open door.

"Thank you," Brooke replied, stepping in and walking past me, the delicious woody scent of her perfume lingering in the air behind her. I shut the door and directed her towards the living room.

"Have a seat," I said, gesturing towards the couch. Dropping her duffel bag to the floor, she lowered herself to the couch, making herself comfortable.

"Would you like anything to drink?" I asked, still reeling from the embarrassment of just a few minutes earlier.

"Some water would be fine," she spoke, flashing another smile that sent a flash of heat directly from the pit of my stomach into places it definitely shouldn't be in.

"Coming right up." I turned and slowly headed towards the kitchen. I could feel her eyes piercing through the skin of my back, making my knees wobbly. *As if they needed to be any more wobbly.* I walked to the top right cabinet, pulled out a glass, and poured in some cold water from the water dispenser on the fridge door. The cold on my skin helped me regain my composure as I walked back into the living room. Placing the glass of water on the table, I took a seat on the couch opposite her. Her eyes wandered across the room as she took a few sips before finally landing squarely on me. "You have a very lovely home, Ms. Smith," she remarked, placing the glass back on the table.

Her complement somehow managed to put me at ease. "Thank you. I put a lot of thought into it, putting in as much of myself into the decor as I could. I was trying to get that all-so-elusive authentic touch. It's a shame I am hardly here to enjoy it more. Also, just call me Sloane."

"Okay, Sloane, I received calls from your father and Amira that told me you are in need of my services."

I winced a little, confused before making the connection—Amira was Dr. Alvarez's first name. "Yeah, I need to get into a shape good enough to compete again. I presume she already sent you the file of my medical history."

She nodded and continued to look at me attentively, causing my stomach to turn into itself and that pesky wave of heat to spread all over my body. The piercing gaze of her eyes made it feel like they had a direct passageway into my soul. I swallowed hard before continuing to speak.

"So Brooke, you came highly recommended by Doctor Alvarez. When will you be able to start working on me? Sorry. I mean with me?" I asked, clearing my throat, my cheeks turning a bright red. Seriously, what was it about this woman that made me turn into a bumbling buffoon?

Brooke laughed at my ill-fated attempt at having a normal human conversation. I smiled a bit; her relaxed demeanor helped put me at ease. She sat up, her biceps slightly bulging from within her jacket as she relaxed into the seat. "We are going to do a mix of stretching exercises, massage therapy, strengthening single leg work as we build strength to full weight bearing again as well incorporating both ice and heat therapy techniques. I will start working *with* you when you are ready."

I blushed again at her cheeky play on my words. "Well, I'm ready, and you're already here, so how about right now?"

Brooke nodded, her gorgeous locks moving in sync with the motion of her head. "Yes, that's perfectly fine by me. Well then, for today's session, I will assess you, then I will determine the means with which we will use the techniques I mentioned earlier." She unzipped her duffel bag and took out a tiny pink notebook—which quite surprised me—and pen.

"Do you have a specific place we can work in or is here okay?"

"This will do for today, but I'll have the

gym prepared before you come over for our next session," I replied quite meekly.

She nodded before getting up on her feet, removing an exceptionally large blue yoga mat from her duffel bag and spreading it flat on the ground. "Lie down here. The first thing I will do is assess your leg. Is that okay?" I nodded quietly, allowing her to proceed. Kneeling on one leg right next to me, she propped up the other leg for support and placed her hand on my injured leg before fully stretching it out. The warmth of her hands sent a wave of shivers up my spine, causing me to take another deep breath. *Jesus, Sloane! Just calm down. She's just a woman.* I shifted slightly as she placed her hand on my knee, applying gradually increasing pressure, slowly raising her hand towards my thigh, then lowering it as she applied pressure to the back of my thigh. I could not tell if it was the injury causing the tingly sensation in my leg or if it was just the effects of the warmth of her touch sending jolts of electricity through it.

"Any pain?" she asked, her blue eyes suddenly piercing into my soul again.

"No pain," I replied, my voice sounding slightly higher pitched than usual. *Only the throbbing ache that has suddenly appeared in my underwear.*

"What about when you walk with the crutches?" The blank expression on her face made her exceptionally difficult to read.

"There's kind of discomfort. My leg feels tight through the hamstring and also weak from not having used it for so long. I mean look at my quad- it is fading away as we watch. It is amazing how muscles fade quickly when you don't use them." I replied thoughtfully.

"Hmm." She bit her lip as she wrote down everything I was saying, causing my eyes to linger on her mouth a little longer than what would be considered socially acceptable. "What about your knee? Any pain or discomfort when you stand or walk?"

"Just a little at times, but it does seem to be improving."

"That's good. Well, a lot of the rehab will be strengthening your leg around the knee to support it and get you back to full function," Brooke said without looking up from her notebook. Without another word, she swiftly got up. I could not help staring at how effortlessly smooth her movements were as she got onto her feet. "May I have a look at the gym?" she added.

"Yeah. Sure," I replied, pulling myself up and stretching for my crutches that had somehow slid and landed a few inches to the left of me on the floor. I could feel Brooke's eyes on me as I was trying to raise myself from the ground, wincing at the slight pain, and I felt even more self-conscious than I already was before. She extended her hand.

"Thank you," I said under my breath. I had to admit I enjoyed the feeling and security of her strong hands on my arm and waist as she assisted me. Her hands lingered for a minute as I steadied myself before quickly dropping them; my heart dropped immediately as I felt the loss.

"Anytime," she replied.

I couldn't help but smile at how blasé her response was. If only she knew the kind of visceral reaction she was extracting from me. Maybe women were always like this around her?

"Please come with me; the gym is this way," I said as I began leading her towards the hallway. Looking over my shoulder, I caught Brooke staring at me, which wasn't helping at all with just how self-conscious I was. Thankfully, the carpeted floor muffled the sound of the tapping of my crutches as I made my way down the hallway. A bright light shone in from the massive floor-to-ceiling windows of the gym. A few pieces of equipment filled the medium-sized room, and a glass mirror covered the back wall from one end to the other. The haphazard way in which the equipment laid around reminded me just how long it had been since I last went in there. "I mean I had the gym stuff all delivered when I bought the house, but I'm basically normally never home and always gymmed on the road or at the tennis club or wherever. I'll arrange for it to be fixed up and install whatever kind of equipment we'll need," I said to Brooke, who was standing just slightly behind me.

She walked into the room, assessing the available space. Her lean body moving briskly as she moved about to evaluate the room and the equipment inside it. I couldn't help but stare at how gracefully she moved from one side of the room to the next, and as if she could feel my gaze on her, she turned, her eyes instantly locking with mine. I froze, feeling like a child caught stealing cookies from the cookie jar. Brooke smirked confidently, seemingly un-moved, before she turned away, resuming her inspection and lengthy mindful calcu-lations.

"We might need to move a few things around a bit so we can create a larger working area, but the space will be per-fectly adequate for our sessions," she said, walking towards me.

"Anything else?" I asked as I slowly backed away from her, walking towards a weight lifting bench and easing myself to a comfortable sitting position.

"I think we should have our sessions every day in the beginning. Then we can reduce as you progress and there will be work you can do on your own that you won't need me for."

"That sounds fine. I will do whatever it takes to get better."

"That's great. First we will work a bit on

strength doing some single leg exercises in the gym so we can get you back to 100% weight bearing. I know your coach has been working on some seated stuff with racket and balls, that is fine, you can continue that just staying seated. It is a good idea to keep your body used to moving the racket and hitting the ball in whatever way you can. I also want to do some massage, stretching and soft tissue work on both your legs. Everything seems so tight and we will need to improve that. Since you have a pool, I do recommend incorporating hydrotherapy," she said as she continued adding more notes to her notebook.

"That's it for today. I should probably leave so I can prepare the details of your routine," Brooke said, not once looking up from the sheet of paper in front of her.

"Okay, I will show you out," I replied, doing my best to stand up as naturally as possible.

As I stood, I could not help but notice how toned her stomach muscles were as she stretched herself, leaving a little bit of skin exposed under her T-shirt.

"May I ask you a question?" I began a

little nervously, hoping she didn't take my question the wrong way.

"Sure, go ahead. Shoot," she replied, a curious look now plastered firmly on her face.

"I know it is none of my business, but why that tiny pink notebook? You just don't look like a tiny or pink notebook kind of girl." I asked, finally unable to keep a hold on my curiosity.

Brooke chuckled lightly. "My little niece —my sister's kid—bought it for me when she saw the disorganized stack of papers in my home office. She said that it would help me organize my clients' work better."

"And has it helped?" I asked curiously.

"Most definitely."

∾

THAT NIGHT, I couldn't stop thinking about her and the way she looked into my very soul with those piercing blue eyes as her hands were on my leg.

But, I knew what my goal was and I knew she was a professional who clearly knew her stuff who was here to help me achieve it. I couldn't risk that. Whatever my ridiculous lust for Brooke was, it could be shut down. Above all, we had to stay professional.

5

BROOKE

I looked at myself one last time in the mirror, trying to choose between my brown and black jacket. This was so stressful. I should have never agreed to it in the first place. The black would have to do. I slipped it on, picked up my car keys, and began my journey by jogging out of my apartment and downstairs to my car.

I walked up to my Camaro parked by the driveway; fumbling with my keys, I just barely managed to open the door. I hopped in, giving myself a pep talk. *Since I'm already doing this, I might as well try to have a good time, right?* Checking myself out in the rearview mirror, I fixed my hair before inserting the key into the ignition and reversing out of the driveway. It wasn't long before the heat started to get the better of me and the sweat began to seep out of my shirt into my jacket. This was becoming unbearable even with the AC on. I rolled down the window that sent a cool breeze gushing through the window. *Much better*. I turned on the radio to find one of my favorite songs already playing. "R-E-S-P-E-C-T. Find out what it means to me. R-E-S-P-E-C-T," I sang along as Aretha Franklin's legendary song flowed out through the speakers and filled the car with her sultry voice.

Checking my watch, it was ten minutes to eight o'clock. I needed to hurry if I was going to make it on time. I stepped on the gas and found myself at The Golden Plate restaurant with three minutes to spare. Walking in, I took in the wonderful scent of the delicious meals all around me. A high-pitched voice interrupted my thoughts, jerking me back to reality. I turned around to find the hostess looking at me curiously. "Good evening. Welcome to the Golden

Plate restaurant. Do you have a reservation this evening?"

"I do. My name is Brooke Miller, but I think It's reserved under the name Janet White."

"Ah, follow me. Miss White is already waiting for you. She arrived a few minutes ago."

I followed the hostess quietly as we walked towards one of the tables at the far end of the dining room. I had met Janet just slightly over three weeks ago while she was working at the gym, and she had been extremely friendly. Ordinarily, very talkative people weren't my type, but Janet was relentless, and that was a quality I greatly admired in a woman. It also didn't hurt that she was beautiful and a shameless flirt. We finally got to the table and found Janet already halfway into her second glass of wine. I kissed her on the cheek before sliding into my own seat.

"I thought I would be the one waiting for you. You look lovely," I complimented as I settled in. Janet wore a red chiffon dress and matching red bottomed heels. Her blonde hair was resting daintily on her shoulders.

"Thank you, but I'm always early," she replied, sliding her fingers up and down the neck of the wine glass. "Besides, I was hungry. I took the liberty of ordering for us both. I hope you don't mind?" she added before taking a generous gulp of the wine in her glass.

"What did you order?" I winced, a little put off by the action.

"I ordered the shrimp. It's my favorite," she replied, her voice beginning to slur from the alcohol.

"I don't eat shellfish," I replied dryly, already starting to feel tired from the interaction and already feeling the need to have an exit plan.

"It's okay. You can have the salad."

If I wanted a salad, I would have stayed home and made it myself, but no matter, I am going to power through and have a good time no matter what. I poured myself a glass of wine from the bottled she had already ordered.

The food arrived a few minutes later,

interrupting Janet's monologue of how bad her day had been and how much she hated her boss. I could barely manage one word at a time before she interrupted me and continued on her tirade. *Oh, thank goodness. Maybe she's just hangry.* In between my occasional nods that only served to fuel her energy to continue talking, my mind began to drift off to my day earlier with Sloane. Obviously I knew who Sloane Smith was before I met her. Obviously, I knew she was hot. But, I hadn't prepared myself for how she would be in person. The deep thoughtful brown eyes that gave away her vulnerability. The honeyed golden ponytail with wispy bits escaping round her face. The calm in her deep brown eyes and her smooth beautiful voice had managed to draw in all of my attention. It also didn't help that despite her tall, athletic figure, the curves of her hips and breasts couldn't be hidden under the tiny shirt and shorts she had been wearing. And those lips, those thick full lips—

"Brooke, are you okay? You seem a little bit lost there," Janet spoke up, snapping me out of my lust-filled trance.

"Uhm, No, actually. I just remembered.

I need to run and get my brother's dog from his place. I promised I would pet sit since he's going on a trip." I checked my watch in faux frustration. "Oh, shit, I've got to go. His flight leaves in an hour, and if he misses it because of me, he's going to freak out."

"That's a shame. I was really enjoying your company," she spoke, placing her hand over mine, giving it a slight squeeze. "I hope we can do this again."

"Maybe?" I spoke as I pulled my wallet out from my pocket to pay what I could assume was one-half of the bill.

Janet eyed the amount as I started to close and put away my wallet. "I actually forgot my wallet at home. Could you cover the rest? Next time is on me. I promise." A meek smile appeared on her face.

"Sure." I faked a smile and placed the rest of the bills on the table.

"Alright, goodbye."

"Bye, Janet," I said, rolling my eyes as I turned and walked away.

The fifteen-minute ride back home was silent. I just wasn't in the mood for music anymore. *I should have just stayed home and binged on a tv show.* Shutting the door behind me, I placed my keys and wallet in a bowl by the door. *Dating really shouldn't be this difficult.* I took off my jacket and headed towards the fridge, where I took out a cold beer and some ham to make a sandwich that would have to do as dinner.

Taking a sip, I picked my phone and dialed Deja's number. It rang twice before I heard her warm voice on the other side, "You honestly do have the worst timing, B."

"Well, nice to talk to you too. What did I do this time?"

"The episode of *Fixers* I'm watching is just getting good, and to be honest, tonight's mac and cheese is absolutely divine. I'm pretty sure this is what heaven feels like."

"Oh man, now I want mac and cheese. I should have passed by tonight."

"Aren't you supposed to be on a date with that girl from your gym you told me about?"

"Short story; it was a bust. Long story; I might need a new gym," I replied, leaning over my kitchen counter and taking a sip of my beer.

"What happened, Brooke?"

I sighed and took another gulp before continuing, "Janet just couldn't stop talking. She complained about her colleagues and her boss the whole damn night. I couldn't even get a word in."

"C'mon, Brooke, cut her some slack; maybe she was just having a rough day."

"She also ordered shellfish for me before I got there, told me to eat a salad, and claimed she left her wallet at home."

"Who orders for you on your first date? Also, that wallet shtick is really getting old. Then what happened?" she asked, her voice clearly muffled by the mac and cheese she was eating.

"I told her I had to go pet sit for my brother," I laughed.

"But he lives in Chicago," Deja blurted out mid-laughter.

"She doesn't know that."

"That's a good excuse. I'm saving it for a rainy day."

I paused for a minute before responding. "I am done putting myself out there. This was the final blow for me," I replied.

"Two weeks. I'm giving you two weeks, and you'll be hitting on some random woman on the street," she replied as I swallowed my last gulp.

"Nope. I'm over it. Done," I replied defiantly.

"I'll bet you 50 bucks. You won't last a week."

The thought of Sloane's endless smooth tan legs shot through my mind. I remembered how they felt under my hands. I shook my head.

I glanced at the watch still on my wrist. It was getting late. "Your lack of belief in me hurts my feelings. Anyway, I should be going now. I have to be up early tomorrow morning, and that whole Janet situation just drained all the energy out of my body. Besides, I do not want to be the reason you have indigestion tomorrow, considering I know you're not chewing your food properly," I teased.

"Shut up. Goodnight, Brooke."

"Goodnight, Dej," I said and quickly hung up the phone.

After that conversation, I realized just how tired I was. I put the ham back into the fridge; the heavy lunch I ate would, unfortunately, have to do as dinner for this evening. I walked into my room, drawing the curtains that previously allowed the intense light from the full moon outside into the room. I took off my clothes and slid into the warmth of my bed. Bedtime had always been my favorite time of day.

As I lay in the dark and quiet, all I could think about was Sloane Smith. Her smile remained etched into my memory and lulled me into the most peaceful sleep I had in a while. I don't know what it was about her, I knew it was impossible for us ever to be together because of my job and who knew if she was even into women? I needed to stay professional. But the calmness and warmth she exuded drew me in.

All I knew is that for the first time in a long time, I was excited to go to work, and that was good enough for me.

6

SLOANE

"Well, you seem to be glowing compared to the last time I saw you," Tiffany said, sipping on a glass of iced tea as she stretched herself out on the chair.

"I feel great, better than ever. It's been two months now working with Brooke, and I'm getting way better. I no longer need crutches, I barely have a limp, and the pain is very minimal. I can start running again soon," I replied, taking a few steps to my seat.

"I couldn't be any prouder of you. You deserve it, Sloane." A tiny smile formed on her lips.

"Thanks, Tiff." I turned my attention to the watch on my wrist. "I really do look forward to having physical therapy sessions nowadays. In fact, Brooke should be here any minute." I couldn't help smiling at the thought.

"And would I be mistaken if I blamed the hot physiotherapist for that schoolgirl smile you have on your face right now?" Tiffany responded in her usual cheeky manner.

"Tiff!" I responded, mortified. My desire for Brooke couldn't be that obvious, could it?

"Hey, I'm no genius, but I know sexual tension when I see it."

"Nothing has happened, Tiff, plus Brooke is a professional; I don't think she would risk her reputation just for me," I responded slowly, not entirely sure whether it was Tiffany or myself I was trying to convince.

I was about to continue with my defense when the ring of the doorbell echoed through the living room, bringing our conversation to a halt.

"Right on time," Tiffany said, a devilish smile on her face.

"You shut up." I scowled at Tiffany, now feeling a heightened sense of self-consciousness as I walked towards the door.

I took a deep breath before opening the door. Brooke walked in, a broad smile on her face. *God, this woman was capable of lighting up a room without even trying.* "Morning, Sloane."

"Hi Brooke," I responded as I closed the door, trying my best to calm down the usual rise in my heart rate whenever she was around. I had just started my go-to small talk when Tiffany spoke up, cutting me short.

"So, you're the beautiful and hardworking physiotherapist my friend just hasn't been able to shut up about." I turned around to find a slightly confused Brooke being led towards the couch by a determined Tiffany.

"Tiff!" I scowled, wide-eyed, trying my best to hide my annoyance.

I walked a few steps towards them as I spoke. "Brooke, this is Tiffany, my best friend."

"Nice to meet you, Tiffany." Brooke smiled, evidently still a little surprised by Tiffany's forthrightness.

"Tiffany was just leaving."

"Nice biceps, Brooke." Tiffany winked at her. Brooke just looked bemused.

Tiffany flashed me a devilish grin before letting go of Brooke's arm and picking up her bag. "Oh, I almost forgot about my appointment." The tone in her voice was almost as fake as the smile she directed at me. "It was great meeting you, Brooke. I hope my friend here doesn't wait around too long to invite you out for a meal or a night out on the town with us."

I rolled my eyes. "Let me walk you to the door, Tiff."

Brooke smiled and shook Tiffany's hand. "It was a pleasure meeting you, Tiffany. Sloane, I'll be in the gym," she said, leaving the room.

Tiffany followed Brooke with her eyes until she had turned into the corridor before quickly turning her attention back to me. "Would you two just make out already! I can see the eyes you're making at each other."

"Oh, come on, Tiff. I told you it's not even like that."

"Well, you better make it like that because she is gorgeous."

"I don't even know if she's single," I retorted, allowing myself to see the possibility for a minute.

Tiffany raised her eyebrow. "Even if she's not, you can still try and get her."

I couldn't help but laugh as I gave her a final hug. "Thank you for visiting, Tiffany."

"You're welcome. Now stop being a little coward and go ask that hot woman out."

"Okay. Okay. Bye," I responded as I opened the door for her to leave. I paused for a few moments as I watched Tiffany walk to her car. I definitely needed them if I was going to be able to get through the session with Brooke

I walked in the direction of the gym; as I got closer, the rhythmic clinging of metal got louder. The door slightly open, I notice Brooke sitting on the bench in a sports bra pulling weights, her back muscles flexing with every pull. She was already working up a sweat. I pushed the door open; the light creaking of the hinges broke Brooke's concentration, causing her to turn her attention towards me. "I decided to squeeze in a workout as I waited for you to finish up with your friend. I hope you don't mind," she said, putting the weight back in its place before turning towards me.

I walked towards the physio table and lifted myself as gracefully as I could onto it. I was wearing my little lycra shorts I always liked to wear when training at home. I saw Brooke's eyes stray to my legs. "Anytime. Help yourself."

Brooke nodded slowly before continuing, "I'm just going to do some mobility work with your leg," she said, walking towards me, finally stopping right next to the table. She took hold of my leg, the warmth of her hands spreading a warm feeling on my skin, causing me to take a deep breath.

"Tell me if you feel uncomfortable, Okay?"

I nodded as I relaxed onto the table; the kindness in Brooke's blue eyes always made me feel at ease. She stood next to my waist and took hold of my leg, bending it slightly at first, paying attention to my body language. I was totally fine; the past few months had worked wonders for me. She continued, bending and stretching it out even further—still, nothing. I was perfectly fine. I watched closely as a tiny smile began to form on Brooke's face.

"It's looking pretty good."

I nodded absent-mindedly; my eyes remained transfixed on her. On the table, I got my chance to study her face fully. She tightened her jaw as she concentrated, adding more definition to her already razor-sharp jawline. A slight wrinkle formed across her forehead whenever she was in deep thought. Her flawless skin was always glowing; I couldn't bring myself to look away.

"OK, I'm just going to do some soft tissue work on both your legs. Try and relax."

I was lost in another world for the next hour as her magical hands travelled all over my legs.

"Earth to Sloane. Can you hear me?"

Brooke's words shook me out of my trance; my gaze shifted to her eyes to find her looking directly at me.

"Yeah," I responded, my cheeks turned

slightly red; I hoped she didn't notice the staring.

"It's time to get down and we will do some single squats with the box here."

I nodded shyly, still a little embarrassed, before quickly getting off the table.

"Ok, slowly down to the box, pause on the box and then back up." Brooke spoke as she demonstrated. I did five sets of squats as she requested before I made a face- my legs were getting tired; I still didn't have the strength I used to have.

Brooke instantly noted my reaction and stretched out her arm; I took hold of it and pulled myself up. Now a little tired, I wobbled a little; I felt my legs give in and was just about to fall when I felt the warmth of Brooke's hands on my waist, steadying me. I felt a sudden bolt of electricity run through me.

"I think that's enough for today. I know you are doing some tennis stuff with your coach tomorrow. I don't want to push you too hard. Make sure you are just standing or walking tomorrow. NO running. Promise?" Brooke spoke from behind me, her breath warming the back of my neck. I stood still for a moment, transfixed by how good this felt when Brooke suddenly let go. I felt my heart drop immediately with the sense of loss. I took a deep breath and turned around to find her gathering her things. She zipped up her duffel bag and placed her jacket on her shoulder. "Take it easy on the leg. It's clear it is getting better, but we aren't 100 percent there just yet, okay?"

"Okay."

"I'll just show myself out, then. Bye, Sloane," Brooke said cheerfully, her eyes dancing as she smiled.

I nodded. I watched as she walked away, confidently waltzing to the door. For some reason, I felt a weight in my stomach; I couldn't bear it. Against my better judgment, I spoke up. "Brooke, would you like to stay for dinner?"

She stopped right at the door and turned back to face me, a mixture of what seemed like confusion and amusement on her face. "Isn't it a little early for dinner?"

"How about a drink then?" I persisted; the source of this newfound confidence entirely unknown to me.

Her eyes dropped to the watch on her already outstretched arm. "It's only three o'clock. Plus, I have another session with a client in an hour."

"Well, it's five o'clock somewhere. Come on; just one drink won't hurt."

Brooke leaned on the doorway, seemingly considering the idea. "Okay, fine. But just one. I can't be late."

"You won't. I promise," I replied as I walked towards her. Brooke allowed me to pass her and followed slowly behind me as I walked over to the kitchen.

"I have beer and wine. What's your poison?"

Brooke pulled out a high black stool from under the marble counter's edge. "I'll have a beer." I pulled the fridge door open, taking out a bottle of beer and the remainder of half a bottle of Rosé, and placed them on the counter. I wasn't really much of a drinker. I never touched it in competition season, but here at home, with tennis approaching imminently it seemed every bit a normal adult thing to do, to have a glass of wine with dinner on occasion. I walked over to the opposite end of the kitchen and grabbed the bottle opener from one of the drawers, handing it to Brooke; the tips of her fingers slowly brushing over my hands as she took hold of it. "Thank you," she said softly as she keenly watched my movements.

I turned to get the glasses from the top cabinet. I stood on my toes to reach, but I couldn't quite reach. I wobbled unsteadily.

"Let me try," Brooke said as she got off her stool and began walking towards me. I turned in an effort to move aside, but she was a second too fast, trapping me between her and the sink behind me. The sudden contact made my body freeze, completely unable to move. I took a deep breath, inhaling the scent of her musky cologne.

"I'm sorry." Brooke smiled nervously as she drove her fingers through her thick hair. I stepped aside and watched as she stretched for the glasses, her flawless skin tanned from the Miami sun. The perfect curvature of her full pink lips and the wrinkles at the end of her blue eyes stood out as she stood in front of me, handing me the retrieved glass. Unable to stop myself, I placed one hand on her waist. The feeling of her well-defined muscles through her black t-shirt was incredibly sexy.

Brooke stood silently in front of me, her eyes never leaving mine; they shone brightly, almost as if daring me to make a move. My heart thrumming wildly, I closed my eyes, pulled her in, and kissed her. A part of me was expecting her to step back, but to my surprise, she kissed me back. At first, gently, tenderly, and then more deeply, hungrily. Brooke's hand caressed my back, pulling me even closer into her, causing her breasts to brush against mine and un-leashing a wave of aching arousal throughout my body. I went up on my toes for better access; I didn't want it to stop. I wanted to be lost in this fantasy. This fantasy that felt like an untamed fire within me. I ran my tongue across Brooke's lower lip when the harsh shattering of glass thrust me back to reality. Shocked, I broke the kiss to find that pieces of the wine glass Brooke had dropped were scattered all over the floor.

"I'm so sorry. Let me clean this up before anyone gets hurt," Brooke said, pan-icking but still holding on to my waist.

I ran my thumb down her cheek. Her worried face looked cuter than I thought it would. "No, it's okay. I will clean it up," I said as I squatted to the floor and began to pick up the bigger pieces.

Brooke squatted right next to me and held my hand, urging me to stand. "I am sorr—"

"It's okay. These things happen," I interrupted her. "Besides, it's not a party unless something breaks."

"It's not just the glass, Sloane. I shouldn't have kissed you. The kiss was great, I liked it, but it should not have happened. I am a professional, and this is my work. I should not be kissing you. This was a mistake," Brooke paused to look at me, a sad look in her eye, "I should probably get going."

My heart sank as I watched her walk towards the couch, pick up her bag and leave.

7

I put my beer down on the kitchen counter and continued to pace through my living room. What was that? What just happened? I had barely managed to get through my session with Mr. Rodgers. Sure, I had had clients hit on me before, but never had I ever had such an intense yearning for any of them; well, until Sloane Smith, the big tennis star. I walked back to my counter, picked up my beer, and took another sip. It had been three hours since I left her house, and I couldn't get her out of my mind; the softness of her lips, the warmth of her body, and the fire of that kiss. I walked over to the couch and took another sip as I sat. I picked up my phone and called Deja. The ominous ringing seemed to make the beating of my heart somehow more prominent.

"B," her voice finally came through.

"Code red! Code red!"

"What's up?" I could already hear the concern in Deja's voice.

I sank into my chair. "I kissed Sloane today."

"Sloane? Sloane Smith? The hotshot tennis star you're supposed to be helping with therapy?"

"Yup," I spoke as I took another huge gulp of my drink. "Well, she kissed me, and I sort of kissed her back."

"I knew it! More girl drama. Side note: You owe me 50 bucks."

I rolled my eyes at her cockiness; either way, she had been right after all. "This is bad, Dej. Like, really bad. Should I quit? Get her a replacement?"

Deja paused for a moment, taking in what I was saying. "So, what's the big deal? It's not like you're a thirteen-year-old who just had her first kiss."

"The problem is, I wanted to kiss her

back. I've been thinking about kissing her since the first time we met, and, well, uh, a *lot* more." I sighed, taking in the gravity of my words. I hadn't admitted this to anyone before, not even myself.

There was a long silence on the other end. "So, you genuinely like this woman?"

"I do."

"Then why on earth would you quit?"

"Because that is the professional thing to do. Isn't it?"

"But you just said that you want to kiss her again."

"I don't want to be that person who sleeps around with their clients. Isn't there a saying about doing the do where you eat?"

"Oh, Come on, Brooke, You're both consenting adults. I don't see why you can't work it out. You can still be professional and have a little fun."

I was silent for a minute, considering it. Deja was right. Clearly, Sloane wanted this as much as I did. I had felt the heat of her desire in her kiss. We could be adults about this. "Alright, I will think about it."

"That's my girl. Just have some fun and

see where it takes you. You of all people know how to have a good time."

I could hear the mischief in her voice. Yes, I liked to have a good time, especially after the divorce. And girls definitely enjoyed going out with me, so what was the harm? "Alright. Alright, that's enough. I get it."

"Good, because I have an early meeting tomorrow, and I am only half done preparing for it. So, I've got to go."

"I'll let you finish up. Thanks for the perspective."

"Goodnight B."

"Goodnight."

8

SLOANE

I sighed and put down the copy of Ashley Nelson's *The Wilds* that I was trying—and failing—to read. It had been almost an hour, and I had barely covered ten pages. It had been over twenty-four hours, and I hadn't heard anything from Brooke. *I shouldn't have done that. I messed it up.* I sat up and stared at my reflection in the darkness of the television screen. *This isn't good. Maybe I should apologize.* I picked up my phone and unlocked it. I quickly scrolled through the phone book until I got to Brooke's contact. I didn't have the guts to call; maybe I should just text. I cradled the device in my hands, desperately thinking of what to say when the sudden ringing startled me. I hoped it was Brooke, and I was spared the awkward experience of having to contact her. *Oh no. Not her. This is the last thing I need today.* I took a deep breath before accepting the call.

"What do you want, Celine?"

"Hey, Sloane. Long time, huh?"

"Yeah, well, that's on you, isn't it?

"I know, Sloane, I'm sorry, but I just want us to talk to you. Can we meet? Please."

"I have nothing to say to you. Plus, didn't you leave the state to be with that bimbo you cheated with?

"I know what I did was unforgivable, but please give me a chance to apologize. Things between her and me are over. I moved back like two months ago. I just need twenty minutes, please, Sloane."

I sat back in my chair; this is something I definitely didn't see coming. But I needed something, anything, to take my mind away from the situation with Brooke. They say better the devil you know, right? "How does an hour from now sound?"

"That's fine."

"Let's meet at The Detour Coffee House."

"Alright. See you then."

Driving to the café in my Jeep, I could not even believe myself. Here I was going to meet with Celine on a whim after two years. Celine was another tennis player on the circuit and had been my girlfriend for three years until she cheated and left me for yet another tennis player. She hadn't even been sorry. At least it didn't seem like she was based on the measly apology and moving to go be with her on the other side of the country. She claimed she loved Yulia, and who was I to stand in the way of that? It had been brutal. I had hadn't really been in a serious relationship before. And although this one had been top secret from both the other players and the press, Celine and her infidelity broke me. I couldn't get out of bed for weeks. Nothing could fill the Celine-shaped hole in my heart.

Nothing but tennis anyway, and I had stuck to it. Placing all my focus and attention on it, and I won. Winning made me feel good; it gave me power, a power no one could take away. At least not until the next tournament. Was it a coincidence she had come back to remind me of my mistakes just when I was falling for someone else? It felt like too much of a coincidence and much like a warning from the stars. I should stick with what I know, what works, and that was tennis, not love or dating. Those things hurt, and I wasn't prepared to get hurt again.

I switched on the radio, hoping that listening to music would be a distraction from the growing pit of anxiety at the bottom of my stomach. I pulled up into the parking lot, switching off the engine before I stepped out of the car.

I cannot believe I'm doing this. I pushed the coffee shop door open, inhaling the delicious aroma of freshly baked pastries and roasted coffee beans. I had hoped to arrive before Celine and get a little comfortable to calm myself before she got there. Still, my hopes were immediately dashed when I noticed Celine sitting by the window sipping what I could only assume was a decaf. She liked drinking it when she has an early morning or when she is nervous, and I hated the fact that I still remembered that about her. I had a surge of mixed feelings as I walked up to her—anger, hurt, and yet a weird sense of curiosity. It bugged me that I needed answers, but I did. Celine noticed my presence and smiled weakly as I slid into the booth opposite her.

"Hi, Sloane. Glad you could make it," she said as she took a sip of her coffee.

"Hey." I spoke simply, unsure of how to go about this or even what I was doing there. We sat in a thick air of uncomfortable silence until a slender waitress in her early twenties walked up to our table. "Good evening, ma'am. What would you like to have?" she said to me.

Feeling slightly relieved, I looked up at her. The tag pinned to her blue polo shirt read *Mary*. "I'll take an iced coffee in a to-go cup, please." Her face twisted as she quickly scribbled the order into her white notebook and left. I turned my attention back to Celine; she hadn't changed much. Her hair was trimmed to shoulder length with the usual blonde highlights. She was in her Nike track pants and shirt. She was the same as me and probably every other athlete in the world in that we rarely ever wore anything that wasn't sportswear. We sat in uncomfortable silence, waiting for the other to break the ice until Mary, the waitress, returned and placed my drink on the table.

"I see you're looking good. I heard about the injury. I'm sorry. I know how much it must have affected you."

I took a huge sip of my drink from the straw, suddenly feeling an unexplainable surge of anger. "I'm not here for the small talk or your pity, Celine. Why did you call me?"

Celine cleared her throat before taking a sip from the coffee mug. "I just wanted to meet in person and say I'm sorry."

"I'm sorry is what you say when you spill a cup of coffee or accidentally step on someone's sneakers. I'm sorry doesn't cut it for pulling my heart out of my chest and ripping it into a million pieces." I tried to control my voice, doing my best so that the rage didn't boil over.

"I'm sorry, Sloane. I don't know what else to say. You were always gone on one tournament or another, and I was lonely. Yulia was always there when you weren't. It doesn't excuse what I did, but I never pur-posefully wanted to hurt you."

"You know, Celine, when you're un-happy or dissatisfied with your partner, you speak up. You don't just jump into bed with the next available person."

"I don't know what else to say. There's not a single day that passes that I do not re-gret what I did. It is something that I will regret for the rest of my life. I've wanted to call and meet up with you to apologize for so long, but I just didn't have the courage. Sloane, please forgive me."

"I forgave you. I didn't have to, and you don't deserve it, but I did. I did it for me; that was one way I moved on. So, don't worry about that. If that's all that this is about, then we are good, but I don't ever want to see you again." I made an effort to stand, unable to bear the tension any longer. I needed to get out of there before anything else happened.

I was just getting up when Celine stretched out her hand, grabbing my palm and sandwiching it between hers. "Please don't go, Sloane. I still love you. Losing you was the biggest mistake of my life. I want you back. Remember how happy we were. We can get past this. We can be happy together, again. I just need a second chance."

Celine's words hit me like a ton of bricks; I felt the heat of tears welling up in my eyes. She couldn't possibly be serious. Talking about getting back together after what she did. "You can't be serious, Celine. We didn't just break up. You cheated on me. You destroyed the trust that I had in you. I didn't even know if I could survive that. Why would I trust you ever again? How could I ever be sure that you won't do it again?"

Celine held on to my hand, squeezing them gently before she spoke, "Because I know better, and I realized that I lost the best thing that has ever happened in my life, you."

I pulled my hand out of hers and picked up my coffee cup. "Well, you should have thought of that before you jumped into bed with her. It's too late. I have moved on, and so should you."

"Please, Sloane."

"Goodbye, Celine," I said, doing my best to keep back the stream of tears that were threatening to burst through. Picking up my coffee cup, I quickly got up and started heading for the door. If I was going to cry, it was not going to be here and definitely not in front of Celine.

The drive home was quiet. I opened the windows to allow the cool ocean breeze to flow through the car. I couldn't even believe it, just when things are beginning to get better, here comes Celine trying to weasel her way back into my life. This wasn't going to happen; I wouldn't let it. If she called a year ago apologizing, maybe I would have considered it, perhaps things could have been different, but now, it's already too late. I got home and shut the door behind me; on the brink of tears, I went to bed and cried, bawling out all the pain and hurt I didn't realize was still inside of me from the experience with Celine.

9

SLOANE

The noise from the machine as Nick was cleaning the pool woke me the following morning. I rolled over to my side to check the time; it was already 8 o'clock. I sighed and rolled back onto my back, Brooke would be here in an hour for our session, and I didn't know how to feel about it. I was making significant progress, but my affection for her was definitely going to be a problem. If we were going to keep working together, then I had to keep myself in check. She was a great physiotherapist, and I didn't want to lose her; plus, after the wounds that Celine just brought up, it was probably best if I kept to myself for a while.

I reluctantly pushed myself out of bed and walked over to the shower. As I brushed my teeth, I looked at myself in the bathroom mirror; my eyes were red, puffy, and seemed slightly swollen. This was not a good look, especially not to meet the hot physiotherapist who just rejected you. I turned on the hot water and got under the shower. This felt good as if, for a few minutes, I was washing away all my problems. The injury, Celine, Brooke, all of them seemed like a mirage far away, and all that mattered was the soft taps as the water hit my skin and the fragrant smell of my lavender shower gel.

Brooke arrived just on time, only a few minutes after I was done with breakfast. The atmosphere in the room was awkward as I did my best to avoid her gaze during the entirety of the session. I did my best not to touch, and when I did, I made sure the touch didn't linger. The session flew by smoothly, and I breathed a heavy sigh of relief when I turned to the clock and the time was up. This wasn't too bad, it's not as smooth as it was before, but considering the circumstances, I could live with it.

"You know, this doesn't have to be weird," Brooke said as she slowly folded her mats, stopping once or twice to look at me.

"I'm really sorry for what happened the other day. I promise it won't happen again."

Brooke looked at me and smiled, pausing a little before she continued, "About that, I was caught by surprise, that's all, and I was wondering if," she continued, pausing again to gather the strength to complete her words, "I was thinking that if you're still up for that dinner, then maybe I could take you out on a date."

I widened my eyes, a little taken aback by the thought. This was the last thing I was expecting after our previous encounter and the awkwardness of this session. I turned to her, "Are you serious?"

"Dead serious," she replied with that soft look in her blue eyes that always melted my heart.

"Wait, so what happened to being professional?" I asked, still not sure if she was pulling my leg.

She put her mat down and leaned over, supporting her weight on the table below her. "I thought about it, and I usually am nothing but professional. My friend said I should live a little. So I think we could just give it a try- if you still want to of course. There is something between us. I know you feel it too. Ever since we kissed, I haven't been able to get you off my mind."

"Thursday. Thursday, I'll be free,' I responded a little too quickly

"I'll pick you up on Thursday at five o'clock. And wear something comfortable."

"Where are we going?"

"If I tell you, it'll ruin the surprise."

10

SLOANE

I sat on my bed and considered the outfits I had laid out. This would have been much easier if Brooke had just told me where we were going, but it didn't matter. I was going to have a fantastic evening with a gorgeous woman. Not sure whether it would be a casual (since she said comfortable) or more formal evening, I critiqued my outfits, trying to pick my most versatile one. I tried them on, one by one, and yet, nothing felt right. Exasperated, I began to stare at myself in the white-framed full mirror; my tan was back with a vengeance since I was spending more time outside on tennis courts again. I looked good. I had finally started eating consistently, going out into the sun more, exercising more. It had been a while, but I had forgotten just how good it felt to be able to take care of myself and get out of my slump.

As I stared, I happened to notice the reflection of a beautiful black and white striped dress in my closet. Quickly, I walked over to the closet, pulled it out, and immediately slipped it on. I checked myself out in the mirror; it looked gorgeous. It fit snugly, outlining the curves of my body and accentuating my features. It was short and tight with cap sleeves and a round neck- I felt most comfortable with my legs out so this dress worked for that. I was sure Brooke would love it. It was hot enough for a first date but not too much, and considering that it was neither too casual nor too formal, it was a perfect compromise for the mystery date. The neckline was a little lower than what I usually sported, but it did an excellent job of accentuating my otherwise small bust size. I slipped some casual white sneakers on with it. Heels definitely weren't my thing. Satisfied with my dress choice, I went and sat by the dressing table and started on my makeup. I rarely wore much in the way of makeup beyond mascara but I put on a splash of a pale pink lipstick on and decided it looked alright. I couldn't help but wonder if we might have sex later that night. It would be fast, but I couldn't help but think about it. I hadn't had sex since I broke up with Celine, and I couldn't ignore how Brooke made me feel. I had shaved carefully. Just in case.

I had just finished brushing my hair when I heard the doorbell ring. I left my hair down. My long thick hair which was 99.9% of the time swinging in a high pony, was down past my shoulders in loose honey waves. I checked my watch; she was right on time. Brooke stood at the doorstep; the black jacket she was wearing fit her perfectly and contrasted the pearl white buttoned-up shirt and fitted grey jeans she had on. Her custom white sneakers complimented the outfit perfectly. She stood silent for a moment; I could feel her eyes on me, following every curve the dress formed on my body. "You look stunning, Sloane." Just the sound of her voice sent chills down my spine.

"Thank you. So do you," I replied as I kissed her on the cheek. "Come on in. I'm ready; I just need to get my purse so we can get out of here," I added, ushering her to into the living room.

"Sure," she replied, stepping inside and shutting the door behind her. I walked into my room and picked up my little black clutch bag, stopping in front of the mirror one last time; I took a deep breath. It was going to be a good night. I walked out of my room to find Brooke on the couch smiling at me. "Are you ready?"

"Yes," I replied, nodding excitedly. I opened the door, allowing her to step out onto the front steps as I closed the door behind me. "So, are you telling me where we are going?"

"You will just have to wait and see," she said as she opened the door to her car for me to get in.

Brooke slid into the driver's seat and connected her phone to the car stereo; The XX's "I Dare You" started playing.

I was genuinely surprised. "No way. This is one of my favorite songs."

Brooke laughed as I hummed to the catchy tune. "For real? Mine too." Brooke joined in the melody, singing her heart out while completely out-of-tune. I couldn't help but laugh at her failed attempts at holding the notes.

"You may be a great physiotherapist, but you are a terrible singer." I chuckled, unable to hold my laughter back.

"Oh, I know," she said as she laughed at herself. Her ability to not take herself too seriously intrigued me and made her ten times more attractive in my eyes. "I know my singing is bad, but I'm not trying to win any Grammys. Music is good for the soul."

"You would be a hit at the karaoke bar my friends and I go to," I replied, making myself comfortable in the Alcantra car seats.

Brooke glanced at me for a second before turning her eyes back onto the road. "So, I take it they enjoy terrible, off-tune singing?"

"They enjoy someone with confidence and who can give them a good show."

Brooke smiled but didn't turn or look in my direction. "Noted."

"In all my days, I would never have thought you are a The XX fan," I added.

"Well, Sloane Smith, tennis superstar, winner of nineteen Grand Slams, there's a lot you don't know about me."

I nodded as we settled into a comfortable silence. I opened the window slightly to allow the gentle breeze into the car and watched as we moved along winding roads lined with palm trees, and the view of the ocean got closer and more beautiful. It wasn't long before we got to South Pointe Park.

"We're here," Brooke pronounced proudly as she parked and opened the door.

I nodded as I got out of the car, a little surprised by the pick.

"This is one of my favorite parts of the whole city."

"I can see why." The crystal blue waters, white sandy beaches, and the views of the planes flying by made for a beautiful experience. We walked as cyclists and lovers holding hands passed us by, and Yoga en-

thusiasts and dog walkers stretched themselves out and enjoyed the open spaces.
The salty smell of the ocean was calming in
its own unique way.

"So, Sloane, what do you want to eat?"
Brooke spoke to me, releasing me from the
trance of the enchanting view.

"I'll let you decide. It is your surprise,
after all."

"How about hot dogs on that bench way
over there?"

"Sounds splendid."

I followed Brooke as we walked along
the pier. The sweet aroma of cotton candy,
corn dogs, and hot dogs wafted through the
air, making my stomach grumble until we
finally stopped at a red food truck.

"Hey Ramirez, two hot dogs, please,"
Brooke said to the man in the truck when it
was our turn.

A tall guy with a wide mustache smiled
at Brooke. "What sauces do you want on
them?"

"Just the usual," Brooke responded.
There was definitely some familiarity between them.

Ramirez handed her the hot dogs. "On the house," he added, winking at us.

"Thanks, man." Brooke extended her hands, taking both hot dogs before passing one on to me. After scoring a couple of sodas from a nearby truck, we walked down to a somewhat secluded bench on the beach.

"Oh, my goodness, wow!" I exclaimed after taking a bite of the hotdog. "This is delicious," I continued, savoring every sensation; the tingly, salty taste with a touch of sweetness from the onions, sweet pepper, and the sauces melded perfectly with the soft white bread in my mouth.

"I thought you might say that. Ramirez makes the best hot dogs in town."

"How do you know Ramirez? You two seem like you know each other pretty well," I asked, taking another delicious bite from the hotdog.

"When I first moved here, my brother and I used to come for a run on the beach almost every day. One day, we met Ramirez opening shop, so I decided to try out his hot dogs. I am not proud to say that they have become some sort of a secret addiction or guilty pleasure. The good thing is that they serve as my post-workout motivation," Brooke confessed before filling her mouth with a large bite. It was cute the way she took time to savor each bite.

"I can see why." I spoke before taking another bite. "I didn't know you have a brother. Tell me about your family; I don't think you've ever mentioned them." I covered my mouth as I spoke, doing my best to be polite.

"I don't think the topic has ever come up. I have a younger brother—Bill. He's a neurosurgeon. He used to live here, but he took a job at Woods Memorial Hospital in Chicago. He took after our dad, who is also a doctor. My dad runs his private practice in Atlanta; that's where we grew up. My mom is the principal at South Field High School in Atlanta. Then there's me, the physiotherapist. There's nothing exciting about us; we're the boring, everyday suburban family," she explained as her eyes scanned the beach all the way to the water.

"Sounds pretty great, actually. So why did you move here from Atlanta?"

"I moved for my ex-wife. She got the job

of her dreams here, and I came to support her."

"Ex-wife!" My eyes widened as my lips parted almost imperceptibly. I was shocked. That was the last thing I expected.

Brooke looked at me, obviously amused by my reaction. "Yeah, we got married pretty young. I was twenty-two, and she was twenty-three. We were married for five years, and then we got a divorce."

"That sucks. I'm sorry."

"Don't be; it wasn't anything spectacular. We just got too busy. We both changed. I was always traveling for work. When I was there, she wasn't, and we grew apart, so we just decided to end our misery."

"I totally get that." I clenched my jaw; the story was all too familiar. It was just like Celine and me but without the infidelity and soul-crushing end.

"So, what's your story?" Brooke asked as she smiled, shifting the focus to me. If only she knew the effect that smile had on me.

"It's just my father and me; we've lived here our entire lives apart from obviously all I do is travel for tennis tournaments. My mother died in a car accident when I was five years old, so I don't remember much about her."

Brooke's eyes filled with sympathy. She extended her arm and took my hand in hers. "I'm so sorry for your loss."

"Thanks, but it's okay. I've learned to live with it." I shrugged.

We sat in silence for a little bit, enjoying the views and watching the movements of people who were a bit far off. I stole glances at Brooke; she seemed in deep thought. Somehow the look suited her as she clenched her jaw, seemingly pondering something.

I turned my attention to the water. The calming sound of the splashing waves and the whispering wind in my ear created an overwhelming feeling of serenity. The day could not have been more perfect if I had made it myself. The brilliant blue sky was now beginning to swirl with a mixture of purples and oranges as the sun gradually receded beneath the water. The extensive stretch of water acted as a giant mirror below, reflecting the beautiful colors. I don't think I will ever get enough of Miami sunsets. As we sat in silence, taking in every second of it, I understood why Brooke had chosen this location. It was always more gorgeous every time you saw it.

Brooke turned towards me, looking straight into my eyes. "I hope you're not too full because our next stop for the evening is a tasting event at the opening of a friend of mine's restaurant," she said, wiping tiny bits of bread crumbs from her face.

"That sounds exciting," I responded joyfully, happy that this wasn't the end of the evening for us. She took my hand into hers, spreading an all-too-familiar warmth in my stomach and chest as we walked back to the car, leaving our footprints in the white sand.

Darkness slowly began to creep in as the street lights turned on. The drive to the restaurant was silent, a comfortable, almost intimate kind of silence. It was the sort of silence that felt good. It wasn't long until we pulled up into a packed parking lot just in time to find a group of people streaming into the building. A sign reading *Joe's Scape Goat* gleamed under the neon lights at the entrance. The restaurant was welcoming, with high wooden beams and bronze light fixtures that seemed to bring it to life. The ambiance seemed geared to private one-on-one meetings or small intimate groups. Smartly dressed waitstaff directed us to our seats. The sweet fragrance of food being prepared in the kitchen filled the room. The soft jazz music that played in the background was nearly outweighed by the chatter of people sitting in small groups, sipping on glasses of champagne that were quickly refilled by the servers who were always just around the corner.

Brooke placed her hand on the small of my back, leading me through the maze of tables and people to an empty table close to the front of the room. We had just taken our seats when a young man walked up to us, offering champagne. I help myself to a glass, thinking it might help loosen me up to get accustomed to Brooke's now more affectionate demeanor.

The clinking of glass silenced the room, drawing all the attention to a handsome man in a white double-breasted jacket at the very front of it. "Thank you all for coming to the soft launch of my restaurant." He began his speech by thanking his partners and guests before recapping the journey it took to get there, which was appreciated with a thunderous round of applause from the crowd. "Today marks the beginning of a new chapter, and I am glad that I could share this moment with you. This dream come true wouldn't have been possible without you, so thank you. Enjoy the exquisite delicacies prepared by my team of amazing chefs and me. Any compliments or suggestions will definitely be appreciated," he said. The speech was followed by another round of applause from the crowd that only died down after a stream of waitstaff walked into the room, distributing menus and refilling glasses.

I skimmed through the menu as Brooke and I discussed which of the appetizers and entrees to order. To be honest, there was nothing on there I wouldn't try; everything sounded so delicious. The servers were quick to bring the bowls of sweet potato soup and fresh baguettes we had ordered.

"So, Brooke, where do you live?"

"Why? Do you want to come to visit?" she replied smugly as she bit into her baguette dipped in sweet potato sauce.

I raised my eyebrow as I replied, "With how this night is turning out, who knows where it will take us next." I hoped that sounded as confident as I intended it to.

"I live in an apartment on Coconut Grove."

"With anyone?" I added, curious.

Brooke looked at me, bemused. "Fortunately, no. I do have a dog, though; his name is Theo, and he's the cutest little guy you will ever meet."

The night continued smoothly. Each course was just as or even more delicious than the last. The champagne flowed freely, lightening the mood and easing into various conversations as Brooke and I got to know each other. I couldn't help but realize that this woman was a rare combination of funny, sophisticated, clever, and inarguably gorgeous. As she drove me home, we laughed so hard my stomach hurt. As we walked up to my door, I couldn't help but feel a little sad. Despite our date being hours long, I wanted more time with her. I looked at my watch; it was already past midnight. "So, this is my stop."

"Yeah."

"Thank you for the wonderful evening. I had a great time with you."

Smiling, Brooke responded, "I had a great time too."

We stood awkwardly at the door. If the moment was tension-filled for me, it seemed the complete opposite for Brooke. I stood on the doorstep, unsure of our next move. I was sure of the desire I felt for Brooke and thought she felt it too. The electricity was building as we stood there and looked straight into each other's eyes. My heart dropped as Brooke didn't say much and instead planted a kiss on my cheek before uttering the words, "I should probably go," before turning her back and walking away.

Downcast, I fumbled with my keys, doing my best to try and unlock the door. I stopped for a moment, trying to figure out a way to articulate my thoughts. I turned around about to speak when I felt the sudden sensation of Brooke's lips meeting mine as she backed me up against the door. Brooke kissed me deep, slow, causing my mind to go blank. I lost the ability to think, I could only feel, and I knew this felt good.

Really good. Looking for an anchor, I moved my hands into Brooke's hair as she pressed me into the door; the more we kissed, the more I wanted. My desire for Brooke in that moment was insatiable.

We had been kissing for a while when I pulled out for air. This was new; something about kissing Brooke made me forget how to breathe. Breathing hard, I stared into her eyes. They were darker. I could see the intensity in them. The pull between us was magnetic. I didn't want this night to end, at least not like this. Throwing caution to the wind, I placed my arms around Brooke's neck. "Would you like to come in for a glass of wine?" A cold feeling gushed down my spine as she looked deep into my eyes, almost as if searching for something. I knew what I was signing up for, and it was clear she did too.

Brooked chuckled. "Is that what we are calling it now? A glass of wine?"

"Yes. So, do you want to come in?"

"I do." A smirk formed clearly on her lips as she spoke.

My hands were shaking and sweating as I tried opening the door. I had been thinking about this moment from the first time I met Brooke, but now that the moment had finally come, I was a nervous wreck. Dropping my clutch bag on the couch as I walked to the kitchen for some wine, I needed to give myself a pep talk. *Get a grip on yourself, and don't screw this up.* I picked up two glasses and placed them on the counter. I then removed a bottle of sweet red wine and poured a generous amount into each glass. I took a quick swig before carrying both drinks and the bottle into the living room and taking a seat on the couch, right next to Brooke.

We sipped our wine quietly as I observed her. The silence seemed to only increase the tension in the room. I took one last gulp, for liquid courage, before placing the glass back on the table. I moved closer to Brooke; leaning in, I closed the gap between us. Without thinking, I tilted my head and captured her mouth with mine. Not expecting me to make the first move, she was surprised at first, but her lips clung to mine, engaging in a slow sensual dance. Time seemed to have stopped when our lips met. The raw passion coursed through my veins as her fingers curled around my waist, sending flashes of electricity flowing through my body to all the right places. Slowly I crept on top of her, running my fingers up the back of her neck into her hair. She moaned slightly into my ear. Moving her body under me, Brooke tried to take off her jacket. I kissed her neck, taking in the sensual, woody scent of her cologne.

All I wanted was to have Brooke all to myself, to make her mine in every possible way. Staring into her eyes, I slowly undid the buttons of her shirt and tossed it to the floor. The definition of her muscles was a sure sign that she never missed a workout in her life. Digging my hand into the back of her neck, I pulled her in to feel her soft lips again, but this was different. It felt visceral, primal. Brooke put her hand on my waist, trying to reverse our positions, but I wasn't having it. I needed this. I needed to be in control, at least at first. Pushing Brooke back into the sofa, she made a face but allowed me to proceed. I rose for a second and, without breaking eye contact, straddled her. Our waists moved in sync as I ground myself on her with skilled precision. Her hands moved up and down, causing my dress to ride up to my waist. Her hands finally settled on my ass. She had touched my ass on the physio table before but here she grabbed it like she owned it. She thrust her thigh between my legs. The movement was fast and as intoxicating as this was; I knew I wasn't going to last long as each movement from Brooke brought me closer to release.

I released a soft moan, and as if reading my mind Brooke slipped her hand higher, first on my ribcage, before skillfully landing on my breasts. Her thumb circled my nipples through the thin fabric of my dress, eliciting a soft moan that clearly drove Brooke wild. Without wasting time, she slipped the dress quickly over my head and proceeded to unclip my bra with just one hand. *Impressive.* Brooke's head immediately dipped to my breast and caught a nipple, swirling her tongue against it, sucking. I almost came undone. I pushed myself harder against her thigh, the throbbing from my center now too much to withstand. Without shifting attention from my breasts, Brooke twisted herself and, with her free hand, reached in between my legs and stroked the outside of my panties.

"More," I cried, now unable to bear it any longer. Taking matters into her own hands, Brooke lifted me in full swoop and laid me flat onto the carpet. On instinct, I tugged at the button of Brooke's pants, and within seconds she was stripping off. There I lay, staring at the gorgeous body that I had been longing to touch for so long. My mouth found Brooke's once again as she moved against my body from above me. Her attention moved to my neck, and it was intoxicating, increasing the intensity of the fire between my legs from a flame to an inferno. The ache was almost too much. As if reading my mind, Brooke moved quickly, forming a trail of kisses from my neck over my breasts and stomach to just above the lining of my underwear. Masterfully, she slid them down to my ankles before taking them all the way off and taking her place between my thighs. Without wasting any time, she began to trail kisses around the perimeter of my pelvis, then slowly down to my thighs, carefully avoiding the place I needed her most.

"Please," I whispered. It was the only thing I could manage as I begged and pushed my sex even closer to her, unable to take it any longer.

Ignoring my pleas, Brooke continued to edge me. She blew a stream of air in between kisses that produced a strangely arousing effect, driving me farther over the edge. In one swift motion, Brooke's tongue landed on my wetness, with light, quick strokes that drove me wild, thrusting me to unexplored heights of pleasure I hadn't known before. My mind went empty. I could do nothing else but moan and ride the blissful waves that had taken over me completely. Just when I was about to reach climax, Brooke stopped and began her trail of kisses again.

"Fuck," I cried, frustrated. I couldn't believe it. The ache in between my legs was unbearable. I was so close.

Before I could raise any complaints, Brooke found her way to my clit. She began again, this time with a slower, side-to-side motion. I felt like I had been ready to come for Brooke for months. It didn't take me long; I clutched a handful of Brooke's hair as I came hard and fast. Bursting into new levels of pleasure I didn't know were possible. Brooke moved up and held onto me as I rode the blissful waves that washed over me completely.

"Wow, that was amazing," was all I could manage when I finally calmed down enough to speak.

Brooke looked at me with those big, soft blue eyes. Her eyelashes were long and gorgeous. That was the most beautiful set of eyes I had ever seen.

"I want you," I said when I finally came down from the euphoric high. I was unable to think of anything but having Brooke again. There was so much sex I hadn't had in the years since Celine. There was so much I had fantasised about Brooke doing to me.

"Again?" Brooke asked, amusement clearly on her face.

I nodded, and without wasting any time, she got on top of me again, her warm skin flush against mine. I reveled in the pressure of her weight pressing against me as the hot tango of lips and tongues began again. I was loving the sensation, but there was something I had to do first. Just as Brooke was moving down again, I got ahold of her and rolled her over, finishing back on top of her. I couldn't help but smile at Brooke's surprised expression from beneath me.

"I've got you now," I said, unable to hide the triumphant tone in my voice.

Brooke smirked. "You must be very proud of yourself up there."

"Quite," I responded. I didn't know what it was, but Brooke unleashed a certain power within me. A passion I had never thought I had in me.

Any sex I had had before Brooke paled in my mind. I had never felt the rush of lust in the way I did with Brooke.

We maintained eye contact as I began to slide off the black boxers she was wearing. This felt liberating. I studied her naked body beneath me, desperately wanting to please and hoping I would be enough for her. Slowly, I trailed a finger from Brooke's lips, down her neck, breasts, stomach, and down to her pelvis. Noting where she held her breath, where she liked to be caressed. I took my time, kissing, touching, experimenting. I made mental notes of what Brooke responded to. The nape of her neck was sensitive, her breasts even more so. It felt natural, making love to her. I loved the hardness of her body under my mouth.

Slowly, I kissed her until she was ready. The pool of wetness that formed in between her legs was a clear indication.

I decided I would tease her a bit, so I got back up and straddled her pelvis, grinding my clit against her lowerabs and her pubic mound and the thatch of dark hair.

"I want to come like this," I murmured, I watched her eyes on my body as I continued to grind on her, tipping my head back and relaxing into it. I felt my nipples harden. I knew I was driving her crazy and I liked it. I felt her hands tighten on my thighs.

"God, Sloane, fuck, you are so hot," was all Brooke managed as I increased the pace, my wetness acting as the perfect lubricant. We moved in sync, perfectly, as if we were two parts of the same machine. Created specifically for one another. I felt Brooke reach her hand around, brushing past my ass to touch her clit. I smiled. I loved how much she liked watching me. Brooke arched her back, clenching the carpet tightly as she moaned loudly and began to shake beneath me. I wasn't far behind, releasing a cry of ecstasy as waves of pure euphoria ripped through us, overpowering all other thoughts and sensations. Exhausted, I repositioned myself and laid on her chest. Silence lingered as we brought our breathing back to normal. "You okay?" I asked an exhausted-looking Brooke.

"Still recovering," she responded as she clung tighter to me. There was a soft smile. One more relaxed and assuring than I had ever seen from her.

"We should go to bed before we pass out in here," I said, not knowing if either of us had the energy to even get up and walk the distance to my room. Brooke nodded but was too tired to say anything. Gathering all the strength I could muster, I sat up. "My legs feel like jelly."

Brooke turned to look at me, suddenly concerned, "Not to kill the mood, but I hope you didn't hurt yourself. I know I should have stopped you. I just—"

"Shhhh." I placed my finger on Brooke's lips. "Not tonight. Please, I feel great."

Brooked nodded with silent understanding. I stood up and stretched out my arm. "Let's go."

Brooke took it, and in one sweeping motion, she was up. Without letting each other go, we picked up our clothing and proceeded to head to my bedroom for some well-deserved rest. I smiled as I slid into the softness and warmth of my bed, the memories of what just happened replaying slowly in my head. I turned around, allowing Brooke to spoon me as we drifted off to sleep. It had been a tough week, but being with Brooke just happened to make everything seem perfect.

11

I hummed softly to the repetitive jingle of the elevator music as my mind wandered back and forth between the events of the past few days. Things had been going great between Sloane and me. Sexually, she was insatiable, like a child discovering a new toy, she was desperate to try everything. I wondered what kind of sex she had had before and I figured it wasn't that much. It was as though I had released a hunger in her that had been locked away for so long.

I had taught her to squirt for my fingers and it drove her wild. She would request me to do it over and over. Every time I kissed her she seemed to want more. We had had a huge amount of sex over the past few days and I felt sore from it and glad of it.

I had been skeptical about the concepts of love and romance, especially after my divorce, but somehow this felt different. I didn't know whether it was the newness or the intensity of it all, but Sloane made me feel things, things I hadn't felt in a long time. Some I had never felt before. I focused on the reflection that stared back at me in the elevator's reflective interior. With it acting as a mirror, I studied myself; the black shirt I was wearing fit perfectly, slightly revealing the definition of my arms. I was glad that the gains I had worked so hard for at the gym were finally beginning to show. My brown khaki pants did a great job of highlighting my physique without accentuating my curves, and the black oxfords completed the smart-yet-casual outfit. I hate to admit it, but I had put quite a bit of thought into this outfit. I was going to Sloane's later in the evening, and I wanted to look good but just good enough that it didn't look like I was trying too hard. We had a hydrotherapy session today and planned to spend the rest of the evening together. The thought of it made me smile. Sloane gave me butterflies, and I couldn't help it.

The ding of the elevator and the sudden opening of the door into the lobby ended my trance of self-reflection. My eyes quickly swept through the reception area in front of me; everything looked the same. It had been almost a week since I stepped foot in my office. I had been so busy with the house calls with my existing clients and spending time with Sloane that I just hadn't had time to come to the office or take on anyone new.

"Hey, Margaret, anything new for me?" I spoke cheerfully to my receptionist, who was seated dutifully at her desk. Margaret was a godsend when it came to organizing as well as making and reminding me of all my appointments. I didn't know where I would be without her.

"Quite a bit, actually. We have tons of pending appointments and inquiries for new patients. Everything urgent is on your desk."

"We better get on it then," I said as I walked into the office, a little spring in my step.

Rays of sunshine streamed in from the massive floor-to-ceiling windows as I opened the door into my office. On one side sat my brown mahogany wooden desk with the mountain of files Margaret had told me about. On the other was a bookshelf, crammed with all sorts of books and physiotherapy manuals. I made a mental note; I definitely needed to update those. To the far side of the room was a black leather couch. It wasn't the most helpful thing for my office, but it definitely added to the ambiance. I quickly set my bag down, took my place behind the desk, switched on my computer, and got ready to get to work.

I looked at the massive pile in front of me, applications by new clients, spreadsheets, and reports by my accountant. It was a lot more than I had expected, good thing I was great at working quickly. I immediately sank my teeth into the pile in front of me. I had just become particularly immersed in cross-referencing the office budget for the next quarter when a buzz from the intercom shook me back to reality. It took a minute to register before I picked up. "What's up, Margaret? I thought I didn't have any appointments scheduled this morning."

"You don't. But there's a gentleman in a very expensive-looking suit here to see you. He says he's from New York. I told him to make an appointment, but he's really stubborn and refused to leave."

I sat back into the chair and bit my upper lip. This was unexpected. I could help but be curious, but I was already knee-deep in the sea of files in front of me. *We have schedules and appointments for a reason.* However, who was this mystery man from New York, and what did he want with me? There was only one way to find out. "It's okay; let him in."

It was only a few moments later when a tall, lanky man in what was definitely a bespoke Italian suit walked in. "Good morning, Ms. Miller. I don't know if you have heard of me; my name is Jonathan. Jonathan Murphy," he said as he made his way into the office and stood next to the seat that was directly opposite me before extending his hand. The name sounded somewhat familiar, but as I scanned his face, I could not find any recollection of it anywhere.

"It's a pleasure to meet you, Mr. Murphy. Please have a seat," I said, gesturing to the brown leather seats right next to him. "Would you like something to drink? Some water or coffee, perhaps?"

Placing his briefcase on the floor beside him as he took a seat, he smiled. "No, thank you. I'm in a bit of a hurry."

Returning to my seat and making myself comfortable, I continued to observe him. He had an air of authority about him. From the way he spoke and carried himself, I could tell he was used to the people around him catering to his needs. "How may I help you this lovely morning, Mr. Murphy?"

"Well, Miss Miller, my team and I have been keeping a keen eye on your work for quite some time now. We have noticed your work while partnering with various independent athletes. Your recovery rate is high, and you're one of the best in your field."

I couldn't help myself from smiling.

"Thank you, Mr. Murphy. I try to be the best. But you haven't really introduced yourself, so I don't know if I should be flattered or scared."

Jonathan laughed, a somewhat surprised look on his face. "How rude of me. For a minute there, I forgot I wasn't in the Big Apple anymore." He reached into his coat jacket and slipped a crisp business card across the table. "I'm the manager for the New York Giants."

I was dumbstruck. The sudden realization of what was happening hit me right in my stomach. I took a quick look at the tiny card in front of me. It seemed legit.

"Ms. Miller, you have the skill and the experience to make it big in this industry, and we are in need of someone just like you to come work with us. So, on behalf of the Giants, I'm here to extend you an offer; come and be the head of our physical therapy department."

My eyes widened in disbelief, and for a second, it felt like I was in a dream. It was too good to be true. An opportunity like this could change my life and my career forever. But this was home. I had spent years getting my practice off the ground, carefully curating my clientele here in Miami. I couldn't just let it go. I opened my mouth to speak. "Jonathan, this all sounds great but—"

He wouldn't let me finish. "Before you give me an answer, think about it. If you decide to accept our offer, you will be working with some of the best and most high-profile athletes in the world. You'll travel with us all over the country; just think about how it looks on your resume."

I nodded silently; he was right. It's not every day the opportunity of a lifetime just falls into your lap. Most people would kill for a job like this, but for some reason, I could feel the pit in my stomach begin to grow.

Taking in the look on my face Jonathan began to speak again. "I can assure you that you will be more than adequately compensated." He took out a piece of paper and pen and wrote out something before sliding it across the table."

Slowly I extended my hand, took hold of the paper, and had a look. My heart began to race. His salary suggestion was amazing. It was so much more than what I was making in my private practice.

Jonathan looked at me, a slight smile tugging at the corner of his lips. It was obvious he was getting through to me. "On top of that, you'll get the best medical insurance, 401k, company car—all the works."

I swayed slightly in my seat; all this information was overwhelming. It felt like a dream come true. Before starting my own practice, I had gone my entire professional career hoping for a job like this. And as much as I hated to admit it, I missed being on the road—the excitement of traveling all over the country while getting paid to do my job sounded terrific, but I had to think about it more clearly. I took a deep breath before responding, "Thank you very much for the offer, Jonathan. I will definitely think about it."

Jonathan nodded, obviously pleased with himself. "You do know that if you take the offer, you will have to move to New York. Right?"

I nodded slowly just as the reality began to sink in, New York was still on the

East Coast, but it was at least a two-hour flight away. I wasn't sure if I wanted to move away from everything I knew and loved. "How much time do I have to think about it?"

"The current guy retires in three months, so I would prefer you give me a response in the next 6 weeks," he replied. "We could arrange a trip for you to visit before then, get you acquainted with the rest of the staff and team, see if you fit in."

"That sounds perfect. I will definitely get back to you."

"That's great, but don't take too long now," he said, grabbing his suitcase as he stood up. "Now, let me go on ahead and enjoy the beautiful weather before I fly back home tomorrow." He tipped his hat before turning away and leaving just as quickly as he came in.

I sighed heavily and tried to refocus my attention back on to the work in front of me. I had to finish before my appointment with Sloane. I leaned forward and focused my eyes on the trim lines of text on my computer screen, but it was of no use; my mind kept going backward and forwards, thinking of what to do. On one hand was the opportunity of a lifetime and on the other was the chance of a life with Sloane. I caught myself. I had only known Sloane for a few months, and we had only been going out for a few weeks; it was crazy that being with her was such a huge consideration for me, and yet I couldn't shake her off my mind. She was all I could think about every day at the moment. Her eyes, her smile, her body and the taste of her. I shrugged, trying to push the thoughts to the back burner when I heard the buzz of my cellphone.

I pulled it out of pocket and unlocked it to find a message from Sloane displayed prominently on the screen.

I can't wait to see you, later. XoXo

I couldn't help but smile; Sloane made me happy in a way I hadn't experienced before. I was about to put my phone back into my pocket back when I felt another buzz.

I hope you like surprises because I've got one just for you.

I leaned back into my chair, trying to think of a quirky response, but nothing came to mind. I was so bad at this. I itched my brow before typing up a response

I hope it doesn't top mine, but I doubt it. That sunset was DIVINE.

It didn't take even a minute before another buzz alerted me to Sloane's response.

Well, I guess we will have to find out, won't we? PS I'm not wearing underwear.

I leaned into my desk, a huge smile on my face. Here I was, a grown woman smiling like a teenager, and I couldn't help it. I looked at my watch; I still had an hour and a half before my scheduled meeting with Sloane. That's when the bright idea struck me; I decided to act quickly before the inevitable urge to reconsider came over me. In a few moments, I shut my computer, picked up my bag, and was in my car. It wasn't long before I was standing outside her door. I stood still, trying my best to look casual as I waited for her to respond to the doorbell I had just rung.

"Hey stranger," Sloane said as she tucked a strand of gorgeous honey hair that had escaped from her ponytail behind her ear.

"Hey," I responded. Despite everything going on, it wasn't lost on me that Sloane had the inexplicable power to elicit that warm feeling in my stomach, which I couldn't help but notice she was doing in the moment.

"I wasn't expecting you for another hour or so."

"I realize that. I can go and come back if you're busy; it's just been a weird day."

Sloane looked at me curiously before continuing, "On the contrary, come in." She pulled me into a light kiss before ushering me in through the door. "This is perfect; we can get ahead on our session today before we get down to other activities."

The cheeky smirk on her face told me everything I needed to know. "That's totally fine by me. Perfect, in fact," I said as I walked in and then pulled her in for another kiss. As our lips and tongues tangled, I couldn't help but take in Sloane's sweet scent. She happened to smell like vanilla today.

She had a loose fitting red sundress on. It was the first time I had seen her in anything like that, but of course, she looked amazing.

I remembered her text about not wearing underwear and as I kept kissing her my right hand strayed under her dress to check.

My hand was met with heat and wetness and all kinds of desire as Sloane moaned into my mouth loudly and leant back against the wall, her legs parting.

"Fuck me. Please. I need you to fuck me," she breathed.

I felt a rush like no other as I felt her heart beating faster and her breathing quicken as my fingers slid through her slick folds. I pinned her body against the wall and pushed my fingers into her at the same time as I pushed my tongue into her mouth and she moaned loudly again.

Her pussy seemed to open and pull me in, like it had an absolute and primal need for me. I started to fuck her with three fingers and she went wild for me. Her front door wasn't even closed and neither of us cared. I just needed to take her in the way she needed to be taken.

Fuck she is so open to me.

She was so slippy and wet that I added another finger and kept fucking her, my fingers curled round to her G spot and banged against it.

My thumb slid against her clit every time and it was barely any time at all before I felt her orgasm hard and gush into my hand and all down the inside of her thighs. Her whole body shook with the release.

Fuck she is incredible. I love how much she just wants me all the time.

I held her up with my left arm around her waist and I pulled my right hand out of her. I raised my right hand to her lips and she licked herself from my fingers with her eyes closed in pleasure.

"I totally needed that," I said, leaning my forehead against her and kissing her once more.

"Me too." She sighed silently. "Hmmm I thought we would work first, play later, but it turns out I couldn't wait that long. Work now, play again later." Sloane smiled and her smile was radiant, her eyes were alive, her ponytail was messy and I had just tasted her pussy on her lips when I kissed her. I had never seen anyone look more beautiful, than Sloane in that moment.

I smiled, knowing full well what she was doing. "I'll go get changed."

"Me too."

I checked out at my reflection in the full-length mirror of Sloane's guest bedroom. The light blue swimming shorts I had gotten were the perfect fit, and the sports bra I paired them with was always a decent look on me. I had to admit it; I had chosen this outfit specifically for her. I was excited for today's physiotherapy session; having her near me was always amazing, but swimsuits and water added a whole other element to it. She had a gorgeous body, and I just couldn't help myself, especially with that beautiful smile. Once I was done changing, I strutted out into the living room, through the double glass doors, and out to the lush green backyard. Separate blocks of concrete formed a pathway leading to the pool and the cute little gazebo next to it. The weather was perfect for a swim.

Sloane was already there. She sat at the edge of the pool; her legs dipped in the water. Getting closer, I could see her in a black and white polka dot bikini bra with matching bottoms. They were simple, but she made them look so lavish on her. They were tiny and I let my eyes run right across her body. Stopping by the chaise lounge chairs, I kicked off my sandals and placed them right next to the oversized pink t-shirt and denim shorts she wore earlier. "Why aren't you in the water yet?"

"A little tan never hurt anyone," she spoke while playfully swinging her legs in the water. I took a few steps forward and stood beside her; the water reflected the cloudless blue sky as cyclic ripples formed from Sloane's kicks. In one swift motion, I raised my arms before diving into the water, eliciting a huge splash that inevitably landed on Sloane. "Hey!" I heard faintly as the cold water washed over my body, sending tiny chills down my spine and cooling every inch of my body as I began to adjust to it.

"The water is perfect; get in," I said, shaking my head side to side to get the excess water off and slowly smoothing out the hair behind my ears. I stretched my hand towards Sloane. Gently, she placed her hand in mine, and before she knew what was coming next, I tugged and pulled her into the water. Within seconds she went under, soaking her head.

"You jerk!" were the first words she uttered as her head finally got above the water.

I met an angry wet face. "You look cute when you are mad," I said, unable to hide the sheepish smile on my lips.

"Has anyone ever told you that you are really annoying?"

"Maybe once or twice."

I smiled as I watched her turn and start floating on the water with her back before swimming slowly up to me. Sloane placed her hand on the back of my neck just as she got near me; she pulled me closer, narrowing the distance between us. I couldn't tell if it was her touch or the cool breeze that sent tiny waves cascading down my spine.

"I have to say; you always look sexy as hell in a sports bra. Particularly when you get wet," she said, her lips hovering just slightly over mine before planting another passionate kiss on me.

I reveled in it for a few moments before pulling back and trying to shelve the smile that was now a permanent feature of my face. "That's enough fun and games for now. Let's get to work," I said softly. "Follow me," I said as I waded to the shallow side of the pool, allowing me to stand in the water with perfect ease. I looked Sloane directly in the eye. "I would like you to float on your stomach then slowly start kicking. It will help with developing your muscle strength. The water will form a counteractive force, so you have to be strong and try your best. You shouldn't be feeling any pain by now, but if you do, please let me know, okay?" Sloane nodded as I stretched out my hands for her to hold on to. After a short while of kicking and splashing she stopped for a few long, deep breaths. "The next activity I would like us to do is treading. For that, we'll have to swim to the deeper end of the pool," I said, gesturing and causing a ripple effect in the water. I took Sloane's hand and began to wade through the water.

"Brooke," Sloane called out as she moved towards me and stopped. Her face was right in front of mine. Circling my neck with her hands, she pulled me in for an un-expected kiss. Sloane kissed deep, slow, making me lose myself in the motion. In that moment, I didn't see why we couldn't stop the session and go inside to have our way with one another. With Sloane in my arms, I couldn't give a single reason why it wasn't a great idea, the best idea I had ever had, and with the subtle way Sloane was moaning as we kissed, I could tell her thoughts weren't very different from mine. Unable to help myself, I began to run my hands over her bare thighs, cupping her ass, caressing her. Things felt hazy. I enjoyed the sensation of being kissed like this, desired like I had never been before. In that moment, everything else faded into the background—the session, the job offer, all the decisions I had to make. Everything was thrown onto the back burner; all I wanted was Sloane. The more we kissed, the more I craved. My fingers began trailing over the waistline of her bikini bottoms, undoing the knots.

I lifted her out of the pool and laid her on her back on the side, I was on top of her quickly.

"I want you to sit on my face and make me come at the same time as you." Sloane murmured. She was always clear with what she wanted and it turned me on hearing her ask for filthy things. Of course, I fucked her any which way she wanted. I adored it all, but my biggest pleasure was in giving her pleasure. Nothing turned me on more than watching and feeling her orgasm, she knew it and I knew it.

I knew I would still be wet from fucking her against the wall earlier. The swimming pool would have washed some away, but in sitting on her face, I knew it would be back with a vengeance.

I slipped my wet shorts off and knelt over her face. She moaned as she took me in her mouth and it was the most erotic sound how much she wanted me, having her mouth open for me and her tongue pushing into me like I was her first meal in days.

I leant forward over her beautiful body and decided to use my fingers. Short damp blonde hair was in a strip on her pubic mound. I ran my fingers past it trailing over her wet skin and she moaned loudly into my pussy.

"Fuck me, please, I want you inside me." Her words were lost in my wetness but I knew exactly what she wanted.

My fingers curled into her with the same urgency that her mouth was working with. I felt deep inside her and started fucking her again for the second time in an hour. Her pussy was hot and soaking wet and yet again it devoured my fingers. I could hear my fingers squelch as they fucked her. The angle was awkward for my wrist but I didn't care. Nothing mattered right now except us racing to orgasm together.

I felt her tightening around my fingers and tensing beneath me. I knew she was close. I ground myself down on her face, taking my own pleasure at the same time as giving hers.

I leant my mouth to her clit and sucked it into my mouth as I rubbed myself hard on her face. She probably could barely breathe and in that second I didn't care.

She flooded my hand with her orgasm as she moaned and writhed beneath me and I felt my own orgasm rush through me at the exact same moment and I flooded her mouth with my release.

The simultaneous orgasm thing was a fine art that I had never quite achieved before, yet here, with Sloane Smith, it felt almost easy.

I got off her face and knelt next to her and she was smiling widely, her face soaked with my pleasure.

"That was incredible." Her lovely eyes were glazed with lust.

Just as I was about to take her and hold her the doorbell rang loudly interrupting our perfect moment.

"Dammit!" was the only thing Sloane could manage in the frustration. Slowly she struggled to sit up. "I forgot a reporter is coming over to interview me for *The Tennis Journal.*" A light blush appeared on her cheeks as she spoke. "How about we pick this up after I'm done with her."

"Mmmh," was the only thing that came out of my mouth. I was lost for words. Sloane's tan skin glimmered with wetness under the sunlight as she stood up and tied up her bikini bottoms. Grabbing a towel and drying herself, she walked back to the house with me closely behind her.

"Could you please get that for me as I get changed really quick?" she asked as the sound of the doorbell rang through the house once more, "Sure. No problem," I replied, walking over to the source of the distraction.

Behind the door stood a tall, smartly dressed woman. "Hello, my name is Tracy Hutchings from *The Tennis Journal*. I have a scheduled interview with Ms. Smith today," she said in a lovely southern accent.

"Yes. She is expecting you; come in," I replied as I shook her hand before ushering her inside. "This way," I added, leading her into the living room.

"Sloane will be joining you in just a minute. Do you want anything to drink as you wait? Some cold water or juice, perhaps?" I asked as she settled in the chair.

"No, thank you," she responded, flashing what was clearly a perfectly rehearsed smile.

"Hello, Miss Hutchings," Sloane said as she walked into the room. "Sorry to keep you waiting." Her hair, which was still damp, cascaded down her neck. The red sundress and matching lipstick she wore brought out a totally different look from what was just a few minutes prior. That was some serious skill.

Tracy stretched out her hand. "Hello, Ms. Smith," she said as they shook hands. Sloane took a seat at the other end of the couch.

"Thank you for agreeing to meet with me. I would like to begin our interview if you don't mind," the reporter said.

"No, thats great. Let's get started."

The reporter brought out a black notebook from her bag and a recorder, which she turned on and placed on the table between them. "Let's get right to it," she begun. "My sincerest apology for your injury. Last season was shaping up to be another incredible season for you before your knee injury. How has the journey to recovery been after encountering all of that?"

"Thank you. Well, it's been hard managing both the physical and mental impact of it all, but with support from my family and friends as well as the medical team, I'm doing much better."

"I'm glad to hear that. And how about..." her voice trailed off as my mind naturally drifted off out the window. I was easily distracted by the slow, graceful dance of leaves on a branch swaying to the wind outside. When I finally came to, I got up and decided to change. In light of the change in activity and the obvious shift in mood, I didn't think Sloane and I would be going back to the pool that day. Quickly I took a shower and got dressed in the outfit I had arrived in. The exchange of laughter as I walked back into the room drew my attention to the now-concluding conversation.

"Finally, Sloane, we know just how demanding being a working woman in today's world is, especially a high-profile athlete like yourself. It doesn't really leave much room for anything else, does it? But inserting a little love and romance definitely helps to make life more exciting. I think our readers would love to know if in all the free time that the injury has afforded you, have you had the chance to meet that special someone? A prince charming or a knight in shining armor perhaps?"

I chuckled lightly; the irony of the situation was not lost on me. I glanced at Sloane, who didn't take her eyes off the reporter.

"There is no prince charming, I'm afraid. I'm sad to say he hasn't found me yet. Perhaps I should get a huge bat signal and help him get here a little faster," she said, her voice high pitched and excited. She was clearly doing her best to sell this charade. I couldn't believe what I had just heard. I could feel my heart slipping from its position down into my stomach. I hadn't expected her to tell the reporter about me, but *waiting for Prince Charming? Seriously? Ugh.*

Had Sloane not told her family and friends that she was a lesbian? Or is she bisexual? I just realized I hadn't even bothered to find out what she identified as or what she wanted or in fact if she was publicly out. It hadn't occurred to me before. These were questions I didn't tend to ask; as long as a woman was attracted to me, that's all that really mattered, right? A whirlwind of thoughts began to gather in my mind. *This really couldn't be happening right now.* The reporter's goodbyes drew me from the trail of thoughts that now filled my mind. I watched as they concluded, and Sloane stood up to escort her out. *Maybe I might be overthinking the whole situation,* I comforted myself. Surely there must be a logical explanation for what I just witnessed.

"Thank heavens that's over," Sloane said, walking to the kitchen and opening her fridge. "Do you want one?" she asked as she lifted a beer can, showing it to me.

"Sure," I responded faintly, weighing on whether I should address the elephant in the room.

"That was exhausting," she said as she walked into the living room before dropping herself onto the couch beside me and handing me the beer.

I opened it and took a tiny sip. "You clean up nice."

"Thank you. I try," she responded with a cheery tone that now, due to the change in mood, seemed to somewhat irritate me.

"When did they say your article will be published?"

"It's next month's feature for their Women's Month edition. I'll be going for their photo op in a couple of days," she replied, still bubbly and cheerful.

I tried to remain collected, but the casual back and forth was killing me. I needed answers to the questions on my mind but didn't want to come off as prying. Sloane and I had never not seen eye to eye since we met, and I didn't want to ruin that. As we sat in silence, I realized that I couldn't take not knowing. "Sloane, I don't mean to pry, but what was that answer back there? Prince Charming?"

Sloane nearly choked on her beer. She was seemingly surprised by the question. Her eyes widened a bit as she coughed. "What? What do you mean?"

"Well, when the reporter asked about prince charming, you didn't clarify that you liked women. So, what happened? Does everyone think you're straight?"

Slowly she shifted in her seat as she took a sip of her beer. "Well, yes."

"What do you mean?" My eyes narrowed as I looked at her. I couldn't tell whether I was shocked or upset. The answer was so direct it felt callous.

"They all just assumed I was, and I've never corrected them. I don't look gay. I didn't even know at the beginning when I first became famous; I was just a kid."

I could feel myself start to get heated; the knots in my stomach tightened. "What does that have to do with anything? It's not 1950 anymore; people don't care about this kind of stuff."

Sloane's voice cracked, "Yes, they do. My sponsors do. They expect me to portray an image of what they consider *family values*. They think it'll make me more palatable to a wider audience. As long as I keep my private life private, they sponsor me. If any of this ever came out, I would lose my endorsements and with them my career."

"Don't you think that's lying? Creating this false image of yourself to pander to people who would drop you as soon as they got to know who you really are?" I asked, baffled, my voice now slightly raised.

"The word isn't black and white, Brooke, it's not easy for some of us to just come out. Sometimes it's safer and warmer in the closet, and that's okay. Besides, my family knows, and so do my closest friends, so it's not exactly hell."

Sloane turned towards me, a new sense of blankness on her face. I had never seen her like this. "The world doesn't have to know everything about me. My personal life is mine. I need you to respect that. This is how I choose to live."

"Fine, Sloane. But I still believe the world should get to know you for who you really are. Or at least the person I thought you were. I, for one, would never hide who I am for anything or anyone."

"Well, that's good for you, Brooke. Some of us have to hide parts of ourselves just to make our dreams come true or survive in spaces that wouldn't accept us otherwise. I'm sorry if you can't understand that," she said as she walked towards the kitchen, widening the distance between us.

"Yeah, well, me too. I'm sorry, but I can't be with you if you're just going to hide me."

"That's not fair, Brooke. We've been doing just fine until now, haven't we?"

"I have to go." I turned around and picked up my duffle bag.

"Brooke, wait, I—"

I didn't wait for her to finish. How could I? There was just too much going on, and I needed to separate myself from all of it, and from Sloane, so I could decide what to do next.

I could still taste her on my tongue.

12

SLOANE

The cab driver was obnoxiously talkative as he drove me and Tiffany downtown. I really couldn't catch a break, could I? All I wanted was to stay home and binge-watch episodes of *House Hunters,* and yet somehow, Tiffany had managed to convince me to leave the peace of my house and join her on her Friday night outing.

"I thought we had already agreed, Sloane, no more moping," Tiffany spoke as she applied a little more red lipstick to what was already on her lips.

"Well, I wouldn't be if you had just let

me stay home and eat my feelings away. I'm not in the mood for this, Tiff."

"You won't waste your life away watching reality TV and inhaling full bags of cheese puffs on my watch, Sloane. Tonight, we are going to have a good time."

"Fine. But I'm only going to be there for an hour, and then I'm going home," I said as the cab came to a stop. Arguing with Tiffany when she got an idea in her head was absolutely useless, and perhaps, I did need to forget everything that happened with Brooke and have a little fun, at least for a night.

The Shaker was an exclusive little spot close to the beach and was always our go-to to let off a little steam. They served the best drinks in all of Miami, and the bartender, a very sexy blonde, wasn't too hard to look at either. The space had been converted from an old warehouse, so it maintained a rustic appeal with tall ceilings and old columns. The high-end light fixtures and swanky sculpted furniture only added to the aged feel that was always as strangely exciting as it was calming. Monday through Thursday, the place was part of the mild-mannered bar scene, but come Friday, it was filled with patrons, primarily moneyed patrons from the surrounding neighborhoods. The dance floor always opened up, and the place raged. Unzipping my black leather jacket, I maneuvered right behind Tiffany through the sweating crowds of people towards the table on the right next to the bar, our usual spot.

"Two vodka sodas, please," Tiffany said to the bartender. It wasn't long before she made her way to the table, two drinks firmly in hand.

"How are all these people already sweating? It's barely ten," I shouted over the blaring music filling the building as I slid into the seat beside hers.

"You're the only one planning on wasting your life away, Sloane," she said, laughing as she got off her chair. "I'll be right back; I need to go to the bathroom really quick."

"But we just got here!" I replied, slightly shouting over the now booming music.

"You know I have a tiny bladder," she

added before quickly disappearing into the crowd.

Well, that's just great. A rather plain-looking man in what was clearly a designer suit approached the table. Placing his hand on it, he leaned towards me. "Care for some company, sexy?" he asked, clearly eyeing the low curvature of my neckline.

I felt a sudden annoyance overtake me, but before I could answer, Tiffany walked back over, giving him a stern look. "Shoo! She's tasting the rainbow with me tonight."

"The better for me! It's a two-for-one sale for me tonight, right, ladies?" Both Tiff and I shot him nasty looks, and after a short yet heated exchange with Tiffany, he decided to cut his losses, rolled his eyes at us, turned, and walked away.

"What did you do that for? I was having a perfectly nice time with what's his name," I asked sarcastically, sipping on my drink.

"He didn't really seem like your type, unfortunately. From what I remember, you prefer a more feminine aesthetic—rainbowy, some may say." I couldn't help laughing at her words. Tiffany did have a way of making the most annoying situations seem like a joke.

"Speaking of which, we should get you a date for the night. I think I saw the hot bartender looking this way. If you play your cards right, you could get us a couple of free drinks. Maybe score her number if you're lucky. God knows you need the confidence boost."

Shaking my head, I protested, "With everything going on with Celine and Brooke, I think this player is well played out."

"Brooke? Wait, so there was something there. I knew it! Someone's been keeping secrets, come on, spit it out."

"First, I need another drink," I said, raising my empty glass.

After looking around for a bit, Tiffany finally locked eyes with one of the waitresses. She raised her hand, motioning her to join us. The tall brunette waitress stopped at our table. "Hey, Sam. We would like refills, two Vodka sodas, please."

"How do you know her name? Don't tell me you've slept with her too?"

"Hold your horses, woman. I know I go

around a bit, but come on, I just read her name tag," she laughed. "Okay, now that's settled. I know the empty glass isn't the reason you are so gloomy on a Friday night. Tell Auntie Tiff where the trouble in paradise is."

Tiffany's face was a mix of raised eyebrows, surprised looks, and downright amusement as I recanted the occurrences of the past few weeks.

"So, Celine can go to hell, but what do you feel about Brooke?"

I bit my lower lip; this was a question I was afraid to answer, mostly because I was fearful of what it would mean for me. "Well, at first, it was purely physical; you've seen her. She's hot, and the chemistry is definitely off the charts. I would have to say the sex is absolutely mind-blowing. Like we had a LOT of sex. It's life-changing sex. I have never felt anything like this before Brooke."

"If she's so amazing, then what's wrong? And what's taking our drinks so long?" she asked, looking for Sam as she served a couple of other tables.

As if on cue, Sam walked up, placing

our drinks on the table. "On the house," she said, winking at Tiffany before smiling as she left. Tiffany smiled back, battering her eyelashes flirtatiously before turning her attention fully back to me.

"Look at who just got a crush," I said, suddenly feeling the urge to change the topic. "It must be the dress."

"Don't even try, Sloane. I know you like the back of my hand, now answer the question."

"Brooke doesn't get why I have to keep my attraction to women a secret."

Tiff sighed, "Well, why do you? It's clear that you are into her. You haven't ever even brought this up with your manager. Who knows, maybe it's not impossible for you to show the world who you are and still keep your endorsements."

"I don't think it's the right time. You've read the papers; you've seen the stuff they write. They think I am over. They think I will never make it back. I can't afford any negative press right now, no matter how insignificant. It would totally ruin me."

Tiffany sighed as she leaned back into

her seat. "Can I be honest with you for a minute, Sloane?"

"Shoot," I said before taking in all the contents of my glass. Tiffany was rarely serious, but when she was, she was always brutally honest, and sometimes the honesty stung a little bit.

"I know we hate Celine, but when you guys were together, you were never there. You never introduced her as your girlfriend; you were too scared to even take her out to all those boring dinners and parties you're always attending."

I silently nodded as she continued; what she was saying was true, but it didn't sting any less to hear. "I know it's not an excuse for the cheating, but it was one of the reasons Celine left you. If you really care about Brooke, you shouldn't let that happen again."

"I'll definitely think about it," I said, now wanting the conversation to be over. No matter how much I hated to admit it, Tiffany was right. I had to find a way to make it work. But maybe I didn't have to go the whole way out. As Tiffany got up to say hi to one of her friends, I pulled out my phone and took a deep breath before typing out the text to Brooke. I scrutinized it, checking for typos before sending it. I just hoped she would hear me out.

THE BRIGHTLY LIT lights lining the entrance of The Amber Hotel softly lit the driveway as the car slowed down to a stop. A valet in a classic navy blue double-buttoned coat opened the door and took my hand, helping me step out of the car. I stood by the entrance and took a deep breath. I hated these kinds of parties; everyone was always too formal, too kind, and yet as a famous athlete, you could always feel the gaze on you. These kinds of networking events were a minefield where you could either get your career off the ground or have it spectacularly destroyed in a not so glorious blaze of fire. And tonight, I couldn't help but feel even more nervous. Brooke had somehow still accepted the invitation to be my date despite how badly our last encounter had gone. I was determined to smooth things over and show her that we could still have a fairly normal outing together without me having to throw my entire career under the bus. It was possible to have my cake and eat it too, and I would make sure she saw it too.

A red carpet led the way from the entrance, covering the winding staircase to large, wooden doors with golden frames. This was the first time this event had been held at The Amber, and I couldn't help but be intrigued by the stylistic choices. The corridor was filled with an array of portraits of what seemed like eighteenth-century aristocrats. A friendly-looking man directed me to the ballroom of the evening; it was a large, circular room with a domed glass ceiling and damask walls that made you feel like you had traveled back in time, all the way to the Victorian era. At the far end was a quartet filling the room with soft classical music right next to an open dance floor. I didn't like it. To me, it all felt positively pretentious. I just hoped that as nerve-wracking as it was for me, adding Brooke to the mix would somehow shed a positive light on the whole evening. I couldn't help but admit it as I took in the aesthetic of the room, but the organizers had surpassed even my most opulent expectations of the night with this venue.

The event was already in full swing when I arrived. I looked at my watch. I had thirty minutes before Brooke arrived; just enough time to do the rounds and say hi to everyone I needed to without the awkward introduction. I was going to need battle-like precision if things were going to go my way. Taking a minute to assess the room, everything seemed ordinary; well-dressed guests stood in little groups and mingled over champagne and tiny appetizers. I took note of who was there and did the mental calculation; I had about two to three minutes to exchange niceties with each of the most influential people at this event before Brooke arrived.

One of the servers walked up to me, holding a tray filled with glasses of champagne. I helped myself to one and immediately downed it to calm my nerves before taking another to use as a prop as I did the rounds around the room. Looking around, I noticed Mrs. Stone standing amidst a crowd of people. She was known for her excellent eye and was the first brand executive to select me as the face for a campaign. I was barely out of my teens when she picked me right out of obscurity and placed me firmly in the limelight. Strutting towards her, she noticed my oncoming presence and excused herself from what seemed like an engaging conversation with a dashing gentleman I didn't think I had seen before.

"Glad to see you on your feet, Smith," she said as she observed me from head to toe.

"Thank you. Feels great to be on my feet again and finally going outdoors. I was beginning to feel like a prisoner of my own house," I said lightly. It was all pretty casual, but if I wanted to maintain my sponsors, this woman had to see me and believe I was in perfect shape.

"You look gorgeous, Mrs. Stone," I spoke softly as I raised my eyebrows in awe. Despite how much of a shark she was, I admired the woman. She had an unbelievable amount of tenacity and grit that made sure she owned every single room she stepped into. Not to mention the fact that she was clearly over fifty and yet still seemed to be in the best shape of her life. Her elegant black cocktail dress and pearl necklace matched with a refined set of pearl earrings did very little to convince the world of her actual age.

I engaged her in a bit of friendly small talk before moving on to other small groups, saying hi to everyone and exchanging niceties. I was thankful that my dad had taught me the art of small talk; I could easily entertain and slip in and out of conversations almost unnoticed, which was an invaluable skill if I was going to keep my sanity at all of these events. I looked at my watch; I still had ten minutes and three people left to engage; everything was going according to plan.

I had just turned to one of the servers to get a refill when I felt a gentle tap on my shoulder. Surprised, I turned to find Brooke smiling down at me. I stood still, entirely struck by the visual in front of me. Brooke looked absolutely stunning. She wore an elegant blue pant suit and white shirt, both of which streamlined her figure and highlighted her athletic physique. Her short dark hair swept back luxuriously on her head as she moved with one strand settling firmly on her forehead. My mouth went dry; this woman was so charming without even trying. This was the first time I had seen Brooke in anything other than casual wear, and I couldn't say I was anything short of taken. Brooke in casual wear was something to behold, but her in formal clothing was truly on another level altogether. Just the sight of her in that tailored blue suit made me reconsider the entire party; at that moment, all I wanted was to take her back to my house and ravage her.

"I'm so sorry I'm late. I must have gotten the time wrong," she said apologetically before placing her hand on the arch of my back and gently pulling me closer for a kiss. Instinctively I turned, allowing her access to my cheek but not my lips as I would usually do.

"What was that?" Brooke asked, somewhat slighted. The look in her eyes had me dying inside.

"I just don't want to ruin my lipstick. I ran out of the good stuff and didn't realize before it was too late," I lied. Dying to

change the topic, I spoke again. "You're perfectly on time," I said, trying to reassure
her.

I felt terrible. I wasn't exactly sure if
what I had just said was lying. I am the one
who had given her the details on time after
all, but I would have to process the moral
grey areas another time. Brooke was here
now, and we were going to have a good time
no matter what, just as soon as I said hi to
those pesky brand executives.

"So, how did your last-minute session
go?" I asked, sipping on my glass of
champagne.

"It was pretty ordinary. Mr. Anders is
one of my older patients, so he needs a
little bit more care. It isn't anything I
couldn't handle," Brooke said, scanning the
premises curiously. "How about we do the
rounds? You can introduce me to some of
these people. I would love to meet the
other people you work with."

"That isn't necessary. They're all pretty
boring. I only come to make appearances
and then slowly disappear into the night." I
cringed at the half-truth. Yes, the events
were boring, and I did want to hightail it

out of there as soon as possible, but as much as I hated to admit it, it wasn't the only reason I was hesitant. I just hoped Brooke hadn't picked up on it too. She was about to say something when thankfully, I spotted Tiffany. There were certainly advantages of being best friends with your coach's daughter, and her ability to get into these high-nosed parties was undoubtedly one of them. I had begged her to come. It was my means to ensure that Brooke was occupied if, by any chance, I had to dash off and make conversation with someone else.

"Well, don't you two look cute together," Tiffany said, nudging me; Brooke smiled.

We had just settled into some small talk about the upcoming season when the exact situation I had envisioned produced itself.

"Sloane Smith," a husky voice called out. Turning to the direction of the familiar voice, I met the wrinkly old friendly face of Daniel Wright that gleamed with excitement upon confirmation that it was me. "In all my days, I wasn't expecting that you would be gracing us this evening, especially after what happened."

"I wouldn't let that little injury keep me

down," I said. I turned myself to face his direction.

"Word on the street is that you're going to be back in time for the US Open this year," he said as he walked towards us. Daniel had been a top tennis player in the '80s and one of my idols on top of being one of the sweetest humans I had ever met.

"I really hope so. My team and I are doing everything to ensure that by the time the Open starts, I'll be in top shape and ready to compete," I said, glancing first at Brooke before turning my attention back to Daniel.

"That's the fighter I know. I knew you wouldn't be going down without a fight," he said before holding both my hands, gently squeezing them. "You are a bright star, and nothing will take that light from you. Now, Sloane, don't be rude, introduce me to your friend here," he said as he not so subtly took an up and down look at Brooke.

"Oh my! Where are my manners?" I said, turning to Brooke, who was now just standing by awkwardly watching the dialogue. "Daniel, this is my friend Brooke Miller. She is actually the therapist who's helping me recover as fast as I am. Brooke, this is Daniel Wright, an old friend. He actually used to be a tennis pro himself- one of the very best," I said, propping up his ego. More than anything else, Daniel loved compliments.

"Don't let her fool you; I could still take down most of the people here in a few sets," Daniel said as he stretched out his hand to greet her.

"It is a pleasure to meet you, Mr. Wright," Brooke said as they shook hands. "It's a pleasure to be Sloane's date tonight; meeting you all has been interesting," Brooke said, putting a slight emphasis on the word *date*.

"A friend of Sloane Smith is a friend of mine, and call me Daniel," he said as he maintained eye contact with Brooke. "If you don't mind me stealing her for a couple of minutes, I have a few people I would like you to meet."

"Sure," Brooke responded absentmindedly as she took a sip from her glass.

"Excuse us," he added before grabbing my hand and leading me across the room. Finally, stopping at a group of men that appeared to be in their early fifties and seemed to be deeply engaged in the conversation they were having.

"It is a pleasure to meet all of you," I said, smiling, circling my finger over the base of the champagne glass in my hand.

"Sloane's experience reminds me of the basketball player who..." Daniel's voice trailed off as I turned my head in search of Brooke. I spotted her engaged in conversation with my nemesis Lacy Wong. Lacy and I had been rivals on the court ever since we were teens. What started as a friendly teen rivalry on the court soon spiraled into resentment and petty displays of power as the competition became stiffer and more fierce. We had definitely grown and matured over the years, improving the situation, but somehow, a bit of that infantile behavior persevered both on and off the court. *She was probably in Miami getting some training in,* I thought to myself. I couldn't help feel a little jealous of the way she clung on to Brooke's every word, laughing unnecessarily hard. Surely, what could be that funny? The worst part was that Brooke was laughing too. Was she genuinely having a good time? With Lacy Wong? The world must be turning in on itself. I drew all the strength from within me and tried to bring my attention to the people that stood around me, but apparently, I was too late. They burst out into a round of laughter. Not having caught the joke, I forced myself to laugh along. This was proving way more difficult than I expected. All I wanted to do was spend time with Brooke, but it was starting to seem impossible.

I stood there a few more minutes before politely excusing myself. "Gentlemen, it definitely was a pleasure meeting you and making your acquaintance." I kissed Daniel on the cheek. "Take care of yourself, old man," I said before turning and leaving. This evening was significant for Brooke and me, and it had to go perfectly. I was not going to let it go to waste.

"I see you've met my friend Brooke," I said to Lacy, doing my best to seem genuinely interested.

"Yes, she is just hilarious," she said before nudging Brooke, who sheepishly smiled back. "My girlfriend of two years and I just broke up, so I'm hosting a party next weekend, trying to get back into the dating pool," she said as she held on to Brooke's arm. "I'm sure Brooke here will fit right in."

The subtle way in which she slipped in the word *girlfriend* and the casual flirtation sent sirens blaring in my head. I flashed Lacy a fake smile before turning my attention back to Brooke, "Brooke, I need to talk to you. In private."

Getting the message, Lacy excused herself. "I'll see you later, Brooke." To which Brooke nodded slowly.

"I see someone is becoming popular," I said jokingly. "I'm gone barely two minutes, and you become a whole comedian with a fan base," I recanted, trying to make light of the situation.

"Well, that's what happens when you leave your *friend* behind. They have to make new ones," Brooke responded offhandedly. I knew she was teasing, but it still stung. I was doing my best. I was trying, wasn't I?

"Come on, Brooke, don't be like that," I said, now exasperated. "Let's just try to have a good evening. Now that I'm all done with doing the rounds, I am all yours."

Brooke looked at her watch. "It is getting late, Sloane, and you still seem a little busy here. As a good friend, I should probably get out of your hair. That way, you won't have to babysit me."

Her words sank heavily in my chest, but I knew I couldn't fault her. It was as passive-aggressive as it was true. I was about to respond when she turned around and began her walk to the exit. I stood for a second, not fully comprehending what had just happened. Briskly I walked behind her, trying my best to catch up until I found her in the parking lot, opening the door to her car. "I'm sorry for calling you my friend, but what was I supposed to say? What did you expect?"

"Your date! At least I thought I was," she said as she pulled open the car door. "I'm leaving. It seems my presence here is not entirely appreciated."

"Brooke! Don't go. Let's talk about this like adults. You don't need to go."

"Yes, I do, Sloane. I get that all of this is

important to you. But I'm not going to let you hide me like some dirty little secret."

"That wasn't my intention," I responded slowly, tears now beginning to form in my eyes as the realization of how badly I had botched this whole night struck me.

"Yeah, well, it's too late for intentions," Brooke said as she got in and slammed her door. I watched in dismay as she slowly pulled up and drove away.

The lump in my throat had now gotten much more conspicuous; the tears in my eyes dangled, requiring just the slightest of triggers to unleash a flood on my face. It didn't matter. I would have to deal with Brooke tomorrow. For now, I still had to go back in there and put on a show. "You've got this," I murmured under my breath as I walked back into the party. As I stood at the door, I put my game face on; I was determined to salvage whatever was left of this night. I walked up to Mrs. Stone and the small group she was speaking to. The laughter emanating from them seemed like a clear indication that they were having a good time, something that was woefully absent from my life at this exact moment. I stood among them, trying to listen, trying my best to make conversation, but my mind kept on wandering back to Brooke and just how disappointed she seemed when she left. I felt terrible. I really thought I could make this happen, but clearly, it wasn't working.

Half an hour of fake smiles and the forced conversation was all I could stomach; I had reached my limit of socialization for the evening. All I wanted to do was to get home, open a whole bottle of wine and try to forget everything until tomorrow. Opening my purse, I pulled out my phone; I was just about to call my car service when I noticed four missed calls. They were all from Celine. Not this again. Was there some kind of system from which this woman was getting alerts whenever my love life was in shambles? Already tired, I ignored them and called the car service. I didn't have any energy for Celine or any of her antics tonight.

The drive back to the house was quiet. I just wanted to get home as fast as I could and unwind. The urge to call Brooke was strong, it was eating at me with every passing second, but I would have to fight it. I didn't need her thinking I was any more pathetic than I already felt right now.

"Thank you for the ride," I said, opening the door and leaving the car as we got to my driveway. I closed the door and had just turned when I saw Celine standing there. I stood frozen in time for a few seconds; I couldn't imagine why Celine was trying to talk to me *again*.

"Celine, what are you doing here?"

"I know this is a little unexpected. I sorry for just showing up, but I tried to call, and you wouldn't pick up. I had to see you, Sloane." I could tell she was clearly nervous; she had the habit of rubbing her forearm whenever she was uneasy. It had always been her giveaway. I shook my head, mad at myself for remembering all these tiny things about her.

"It's okay. What's up?" I spoke to her softly; whatever she had to say must have been important if she was this determined to say it.

"Do you mind if I come in?" she said as she shifted her weight onto her other foot.

She was clearly doing her best to maintain balance.

"Celine, are you drunk?" I asked, now a bit concerned. I didn't even need a response as the putrid smell of whatever Celine had been drinking hit me.

"Just a little liquid courage is all. I got here all on my own, didn't I?" she said absently.

"Listen, Celine; it's been a really rough day. I don't have the capacity to deal with anything else right now. Why are you here?"

Celine took a deep breath, perhaps to calm her nerves. "Well, Sloane, I'm here because I miss you. A lot. I can't stop thinking about you. I can't move on. Whenever I think back to the headspace I was in two years ago, I cringe because I don't even recognize that person anymore. I was lonely, and I wasn't thinking straight."

I shook my head. "I'm sorry, Celine, but what does that have to do with me? We already talked about this; I forgave you. We're done." This woman was relentless; where was this energy and perseverance when we needed to fix things between us?

"I made a mistake, Sloane, but I'm here to fix it. To fix us." Celine took a few steps towards me as I watched with careful trepidation.

"Celine, it's not going to happen. But maybe we can talk about it another day when you're sober," I said to her. She was now just inches away from me.

"Remember how much fun we had, skydiving that one summer? Or the trip to England the next year? We were so good together, Sloane. We can get it back. It doesn't have to be this way. I love you, Sloane. I'm never going to give you up."

I didn't like how this was going. Before I could find an appropriate response to that, I felt Celine's lips on mine, kissing me. For whatever reason, I found myself unable to stop her. I couldn't pinpoint whether it was just how rough this day had been or how hurt the fight with Brooke had made me, but I was caught off guard. Regardless of the reason, I didn't enjoy it. The feeling of Celine's lips on mine felt wrong, very wrong. This wasn't even like kissing your friend. It felt inappropriate and uncomfortable; the memories of the pain and hurt she had caused me somehow bubbled up even higher than they had in the last two years. I pulled away, ready to reiterate for the millionth time that I wasn't into her anymore, that it was over between us and she should move on when my eyes rose just in time to meet Brooke's who was now somehow also standing on my driveway, with a bouquet of flowers in hand. I watched as the emotions shifted in her face before going fully blank. My heart sank hopelessly as I watched the bouquet fall from Brooke's hand onto the ground. *No, no, no! this was bad. Really bad.* All of the day's emotions couldn't be compared to the feeling of the sense being knocked out of me as I watched Brooke turn her back and begin to walk in the opposite direction.

"Brooke, wait! It's not what it looks like. I swear!" I shouted, distraught at the awful timing.

She didn't respond and just kept walking away; I was about to run after when I felt Celine pull at my arm. "Let her go."

"No," I said, disengaging and beginning to follow Brooke down the street.

"Brooke, please slow down. Let me explain," I said in between breaths.

"There's nothing to explain, Sloane. I wouldn't have believed it if I didn't see it with my own eyes," she said as she continued to walk away.

"Brooke, please, just give me a moment," I cried out, now completely exasperated.

Brooke stood dead in the middle of the street and looked at me, her normally soft eyes now closed off, almost antagonistic. "If you set out to break my heart tonight, Sloane, then mission accomplished."

"Brooke, please give me a chance to explain. That's my ex-girlfriend, Celine; she and I were done so long ago. I would never do that to you. I swear."

Brooke looked at me coldly; her expression had changed. This was a level of anger and cynicism I had never seen from her. "Don't be rude, go back to your guest, Sloane, you two were clearly very busy before I got here. I wouldn't want to spoil the mood."

I stood there silent, helpless; what else could I do? I wanted so badly to explain, but what was the point? She clearly didn't want to believe me.

"Just as I thought," Brooke said, her voice heavily laden with hurt before she turned her back on me and walked over to her car parked just down the street. I watched, bewildered as she got in and drove away.

"Let her go; she doesn't deserve you," Celine spoke; she was now standing right behind me. In the surge of emotion, I had forgotten that she was still there for a minute.

I turned to her, defeated; all I felt was pure rage. "Get away from me, Celine. I don't want to see you ever again. The next time you call me or come around here, I'm going to call the police. Don't make me have to get a restraining order because I swear I will."

Celine looked at me, a quiet sense of defeat in her eyes. I couldn't stand to look at her anymore and began to stomp away before getting into the house and banging the door behind me. The quiet solitude of the living room and the moonlight seeping in through the windows were enough to unleash the flood of emotions within me. I broke down in the living room crying. This was exactly why I didn't date as a rule. At that moment, I could feel the hurt and pain that was inside me bubble up; I would give up everything I had to not feel that pain anymore.

13

The loud ringing of my phone on the table startled me, causing a little of the pudding I was eating to fall off the spoon onto the pink onesie I was wearing. Once again, I silenced it and turned my attention back to my TV screen. I had been glued to my couch all day, mindlessly watching *Grey's Anatomy*. It wasn't taking my problems away, but it was a great way to avoid them. It wasn't long before the screen lit up again, and Sloane's image appeared on the now-muted screen. This was her fifth call today. Today for our session, I had sent Mark, my best trainee, to go work with her. She had been calling for days on end, but a million calls and texts later, I couldn't muster the strength to see or even talk to her. Not after that disastrous party and finding her kissing her ex-girlfriend in the driveway; where anyone might have seen them, when she couldn't even introduce me to her colleagues as anything more than a friend.

I didn't want to admit it to myself, but I was dying to talk to her, to hear her lovely voice, and look into those beautiful brown eyes. I wanted to listen, to let her convince me that there was a reasonable explanation, but the pain I felt in my heart was overwhelming. Her behavior at the dinner had been hurtful, but I had been willing to negotiate with her. Maybe we could find a way to make things work between us. I had swallowed my pride, and with a bouquet of flowers in hand, I had gone to apologize and make things right between us. That was until she ripped my heart out of my chest and torn it up into a million pieces. I had seen her, locking lips with another woman.

I stared at my screen, unwillingly admiring her picture until it died down again, and the screen went blank. I curled into a tiny ball in my blanket, trying to shake thoughts of her off my mind, but it didn't work. The more I wanted to push her away into the abyss of my mind, the more she showed up.

The growling in my stomach once again alerted me to the fact that the pudding I was having was not going to be enough to keep me from starving myself. I picked up my phone and ignored all the notifications that indicated Sloane's desire to talk before ordering some takeout. I definitely was not in the mood to go into the kitchen and fix myself anything.

It was almost thirty minutes later when I heard my doorbell ring. "Took you long enough," I murmured as I got up and grabbed my wallet from the glass bowl by the door. Absent-mindedly, I opened the door as I dug into the wallet, searching for some cash to tip the delivery person. "I thought it would take at most fifteen minutes to—"

"Hi," a familiar voice interrupted me. My heart dropped as a sudden freezing sensation went through me; my fingers went numb. Lifting my gaze, I looked up and saw Sloane looking quietly at me, a sad look in her eyes that tore through me. There she stood in grey sweatpants and a black hoodie, a far cry from the elegant and well put together Sloane I had come to know. "Can I come in? I really need to talk to you."

I stared at her silently for a few moments, unsure of what to say or even how I felt having her standing right in front of me. "How did you know where I live?"

"I passed by your office to talk to you, and your assistant, after quite a bit of convincing, gave me your address," she replied as she raised her hand to rub her forehead, an obvious sign of discomfort.

I made a mental note to talk to Margaret; it wasn't safe to just give out my number to anyone, even if this time it was to Sloane. "What is there to talk about?"

"I just want to explain what happened that night, at my place, then I will go," she said, doing her best to try and maintain eye contact.

"Sloane, there's nothing to talk about. I

already saw what I needed to see." I couldn't help swallowing hard as the memories of that part of the night flashed in my mind, sending an uncomfortably cold chill down my spine.

"Brooke, please hear me out."

I looked at her for a few moments, at a loss on what to do, before deciding to bite the bullet and stepping aside to let her in.

"You have five minutes, don't waste them," I said a little too coldly as I closed the door behind me and walked towards the couch.

"I deserve that," Sloane said, her tone even more downcast. "There's nothing going on between Celine and me. She and I dated a long time ago, she came to my place drunk, and she kissed me. I did not kiss her back."

"It did not seem like that to me. From where I was standing, it didn't seem like you were pushing her away. Plus, all this drama is just too much for me."

"There's nothing going on between her and me. Please give me a chance; I promise to make things right between us."

I took a deep breath as the sad reality of

where this conversation was going sank in. "Sloane, I am a grown woman, and in all my time dating women, I have always made it a rule for myself not to date anyone who is still in the closet. There's nothing wrong with it, but it's just not where my life is right now. In fact, it hasn't been there in a very long time."

"Brooke—" Sloane tried to interrupt.

"No, please, let me finish," I said, not allowing her to interrupt me. "But I love you, Sloane," I swallowed hard as the implication of the words and the look on Sloane's face hit me harder than I expected. "I loved you so much that I was willing to give it a shot. I was willing to put aside my pride for you. To allow you to introduce me as your friend, to always be lurking around in the shadows for you. But when I saw you kissing her, it struck me. I can't be that person for you, Sloane. I can't do that for anyone. It would kill me inside; I would never be happy, and that's not fair to me."

Sloane walked up to me and slowly said, "I understand that, Brooke, and I've put a lot of thought into it. I want to come out publicly; I'll do anything to make things right. I will do it for you. For us. I want more than anything to be with you. Tennis means nothing if I don't have you by my side."

I looked at the beautiful woman standing in front of me, her face a unique mixture of sadness and quiet resolve. I stretched my hand out and took her palms into mine. "You don't have to do that, Sloane. You don't have to do that for anyone, especially not for me. That's something you have to do, on your own time, when you are sure that you are ready."

"But I want to do it. I love you too, Brooke. I don't want to live without you."

"That's not enough, I'm afraid. After thinking about it, Sloane, I have decided I'm moving to New York."

I watched as her eyes widened at the realization as she slowly let go of my hands. "What do you mean you're moving?"

As I walked over to the couch, I felt the strength in my body slowly fading away. "A couple of weeks ago, I got a job offer from the New York Giants. They want me to be the head of physical therapy there, and I accepted it this morning. I figured that maybe the distance would be good for us."

Sloane looked at me quietly, obviously stunned by the news. "When will you be leaving?"

"In two weeks," I replied.

Slowly Sloane walked over to the couch and took her place beside me. Her head dropped to her hands as she shut her eyes. "Were you ever going to tell me?"

"I don't know. I hadn't made any kind of decision; I wanted to bring it up that day when the reporter was at your place, but you remember just how much of a disaster that was, and of course, you know how things turned out the last time we were together. There was just never a right time."

"You don't have to go because of me," Sloane said, her voice now barely louder than a whisper.

"There's nothing left for me here anymore," I said, feeling the sting of the weight of those words in my chest.

Raising her head, Sloane sniffled quietly, trying to prevent herself from tearing up. "I see your mind is made up," she said as she scooted closer to where I was.

Placing her hand on my shoulder, she leaned in and planted a soft kiss on my cheek. Inhaling the familiar scent of vanilla one last time made my heart sink. I wished I could stop it. That we could take everything and rewind the clock, but it was now too late. Sloane and I were over; for real this time, and the implications of that revelation were too much for me to bear. Standing up, she wiped a streak of a rogue tear that had come out a few moments too soon. "Goodbye, Brooke," she said before walking to the door and letting herself out.

I sat quietly as I watched her walk away, completely exhausted. Mentally, emotionally and even physically, I couldn't handle anything else. I could feel the air around me get heavy and the proverbial melancholic cloud formed over my head. Unable to hold the heartbreak any longer, I released the tears that welled up from deep inside me. The streams of tears coursed down my cheeks as I curled myself into a disheveled heap on the couch, unable to ignore the dilapidating sense of loss that had firmly taken hold of me. I sat and cried, wishing I could take it all back, go back to when everything was good, and everything was simple, but I knew I had done what was necessary, and even if it didn't feel like that at the moment, it would all be for the best.

14

"How are you feeling, Champ?" Coach asked before shooting me a concerned look as we stood opposite the elevator doors, waiting for them to open.

"I'm fine, Coach. Just a little nervous. I'm just trying to get back in my groove."

"Well, don't be nervous. You are going to do great," he said just before the elevator doors dinged open, allowing us to get in. Dan pressed the twelve button that would take us to the floor to our rooms.

"You look more nervous than me," I said, slightly amused. I wasn't sure who Coach was trying to reassure, him or me.

The road to recovery had been challenging, but we had made it through. It had been almost a year since the injury, and nearly four months since Brooke left me for New York—which just had to be the city the US Open was in. It felt like some form of divine punishment, being so close to her yet so far away for my first big tournament back after injury. It wasn't like I was going to find or even look for her in a city of eight million people, but that hadn't stopped the one or two occasional daydreams of somehow miraculously bumping into her outside some store on Fifth Avenue. The part of what I would do next was a little fuzzy, but it didn't matter; it wasn't going to happen anyway.

"I'm always nervous for your games," Coach Dan said, snapping me out of my reflective state. "Especially this one. It's not every day a top athlete comes back out to play after a near career-ending injury."

"Yeah, I know, Coach," I responded offhandedly. My first match was the next day, and we had cut it really close, flying in from Miami on the eve of the tournament, but I had insisted. I didn't need to be in this place that had now become the symbol of what I had lost any longer than necessary.

"Make sure you get as much sleep as you can tonight. Tomorrow is a big day. I need you ready to take on the world."

"Sure thing," I said as the elevator dinged before sliding its metal doors open. The place looked just as nice as I expected. It's not like I had gotten the presidential suite, but I could definitely tell that my sponsors had splurged on this place.

"Goodnight, Coach," I said, walking past him as he stopped at the door of his room; mine was two doors down. I stopped at the door and slid the key card, opening it. It looked pretty standard; a king-size bed, some furniture, and a TV. Quickly I placed my luggage on the ground, took off my clothes, and jumped into the shower. I was ready for a quiet night in, with some wine, room service, and to be in bed by ten, which meant that I had a good three hours of *House Hunters* to look forward to before hitting the sack.

I stepped out of the showers draped in the white bathrobe and walked to the bedside table to pour myself a glass of wine. I was just drying my hair off when a soft-sounding knock emanated from the door. I tied the towel around my head as I picked my glass and strolled to the door, somewhat confused. I hadn't ordered any room service, and it wasn't like Dan to just come to my room without any prior notice if it wasn't game day. Curiously, I stood by and opened it to find a smiling Tiffany at the door. She was still in uniform—a light blue coat and skirt, white blouse, and a killer set of black heels. Her hair was held in a high bun at the back of her head.

"What are you doing in New York? Weren't you supposed to be on a couple of scheduled flights on the West Coast?" I asked, slightly relieved that it was her and not some crazy fan.

"I couldn't miss my girl's first Grand Slam game back, now could I? So, I arranged for a little layover in New York just in time for your game before I fly to California tomorrow," she said in excitement. "So, are you going to let me in, or are you going to stand there and question me all night?" she asked, now crossing her arms across her chest.

"Come on in, Tiff." I couldn't help but smile. Tiffany had her faults, but she was definitely one of the best friends a girl could ask for.

"Now, what does a girl need to do to get a drink around here?" she asked as she sat on the sculpted couch. I poured her a glass of wine.

"Maybe just asking?" I said as I handed her the glass and took a seat next to her. "I'm glad you came. I really needed the support."

"Yeah, I know, Dad told me. He sounded anxious when we talked on the phone earlier, so I told him I would come straight up when I landed, and here I am," she said, sipping on her wine.

"He talked to you about me?" I asked, feeling a little stung despite the fact that I knew it was well-intentioned.

"Yes. We talk about you all the time," she said without batting an eye.

"Remind me not to let you give me a pep talk," I said as I sunk into the seat. Despite the brutal honesty, this felt good, having someone to talk to who understood.

"I thought you must've learned your

lesson by now," she said, swirling the wine in her glass. "Okay, Sloane, what's really bothering you?"

Sipping on the last of the contents in my glass, I placed it on the table opposite us and turned to her. "Well, my first match is against Jane Parker, and you know just how well that went last time."

"I know," Tiffany said as she stared contemplatively into her glass. "Don't sweat it; you've been training like crazy the last couple of months. You're going to absolutely body that woman tomorrow."

"I hope so," I said, the memories of that awful day still playing on a cursed loop in my brain.

"But that's not it, Sloane. I can tell you really miss Brooke. I know you are an expert at channeling any kind of negative emotion into fuel for your games, but you can't continue like this. It's going to eat you alive."

The silence in the room was so heavy you could cut it as Tiffany waited for my response.

"I know, but she made it crystal clear

that she doesn't want to see me anymore. There's not much I can do."

"You could try reaching out; it's been months. She could have had a change of heart."

"I don't have her number, and it's not like I'm going to just magically bump into her in the street. Plus, Tiff, I don't have the energy to that again. I've been rejected enough for one lifetime."

"I know. I just—" Tiff was about to continue speaking when the vibration of her phone from her purse stopped her in her tracks. Quickly, she put her glass down and opened it to read the text message. The look on her face suddenly changed from casual to determined before she glanced up at me again. "Get dressed. We need to go."

"Wait, what? No. You know I have a game tomorrow; I'm not going anywhere. I'm supposed to be resting."

"Calm down. We're not going far. The message was from my dad; apparently, there are a couple of your sponsors in the building. They want to have an impromptu meeting in the restaurant downstairs."

"What, Why?" I checked my phone;

Coach hadn't sent me anything. "Also, why would he text you and not me?"

"I don't know, Sloane. I'm just glad he's actually learned how to text correctly."

"Fair enough."

"Alright, let me go to my room and get changed, and I'll meet you down there in like 15 minutes," Tiffany said as she stood up, placed her glass on the table, and walked out of the room.

The elevator trip downstairs was quick, and luckily for me, it was empty as well. Being short of time for ideas, I had only managed to throw on a pair of jeans and a black t-shirt. Those executives would have to understand. You just don't call a meeting and expect someone to be ready in five minutes.

When the doors opened, I walked across the lobby, right into the restaurant. Quickly I scanned the interior of the half-empty room. I could neither see Coach nor anyone else that I recognized. I was about to reach for the phone in my pocket when my eyes landed on her. Quietly sitting at the corner of the room, Brooke perused the rather extensive cocktail menu. I stood there for a minute, transfixed. There she was in a gorgeous black Armani suit; the soft light from the overhead fixtures illuminated her face making her seem even more stunning than anything or anyone I had ever seen. I was just about to turn back and walk out into the hallway when her gaze rose, meeting me squarely in the eyes. As if having lost control of my body, I ambled to the table where she sat and took my place right opposite her.

"Hey," I said sheepishly, not entirely sure how to proceed from here.

"Hey," Brooke responded quietly, not taking those big beautiful eyes off me. "I wasn't expecting you. What are you doing here?"

"Come now; you don't have to act so happy to see me," I said teasingly, desperately trying to lighten the mood.

"It's not that. I'm just surprised, that's all," Brooke said as she smiled at me. God, how much I had longed to see that gorgeous smile.

I looked around the restaurant again; there was still no other familiar face in sight. "Apparently, I'm supposed to be having a meeting with my coach and a couple of my sponsors right now, but I don't see any of them."

"That's strange. I'm also supposed to be having a meeting with some lady named Amanda Steinberg. Something to do with treatment for some of my athletes. The thing is, I don't know why my boss sent me here when we have a whole team of specialists for that stuff."

That's when what was happening here suddenly hit me. "Did you say Amanda Steinberg?" I asked Brooke, now exasperated.

"Yeah," she said, now raising an eyebrow. "Do you know her?"

"Do I know her?" I could help but frown. I was going to kill Tiffany after this. "That's the fake name Tiffany uses when she's hooking up with random guys whenever she's in a new city."

Brooke laughed, that sweet laugh that was nothing short of music to my ears. "Well then, I don't know about you, but from where I'm sitting, it looks like we have been parent trapped."

"Looks like it. I'm really sorry, Brooke. I

think I should go, but I will talk to Tiff; this won't happen again. I promise," I mumbled; I couldn't help but be embarrassed. It was just like Tiffany to pull a stunt like this. She was probably going to be expecting thanks for this awkward mess.

I had just moved my chair back and was about to get up when Brooke spoke.

"Wait."

I stopped and turned back to look at her, obviously surprised.

"It's not how I expected the night to go, but it would be a shame for me to come all this way only to go back having accomplished nothing. How about we have a drink. Maybe catch up?"

"A drink? Brooke, I have a game tomorrow," I said, now both terrified and thrilled at the prospect.

"Just one drink," Brooke said in that convincing way that I couldn't bring myself to say no to. I don't even think I wanted to. How could I?

"Alright. It's a shame to waste a perfectly good evening up in my room all alone."

Brooke called for a waiter, and soon we

had two drinks in front of us. What had started as an anxiety-riddled evening was turning out wonderfully. Who would have known that just a few hours in, I would be having the time of my life with the one woman I couldn't get enough of? I wasn't sure if Brooke had become funnier, but as we continued to down drinks, I was laughing harder in that one hour we spent together than the entirety of the last couple of months combined. I was just getting myself together from the bellyache of one of her stories of adapting to her life here in New York when I noticed the soft look in her eye.

"I missed this," Brooke said softly, her finger circling the rim of her whiskey glass but not taking her eyes off me.

"Me too," I said, avoiding her gaze, but that didn't stop the now conspicuous pounding of my heart or the heat in my cheeks from the feeling of Brooke's eyes on me.

"I'm really sorry about how things went down, Sloane," Brooke said, her voice lowered; it was now just slightly above a whisper.

"Yeah, me too," I spoke. With my heart pounding in my chest, I extended my palm to cover hers. Brooke didn't move; she did not pull back at my touch. She sat still, looking into my eyes. The air between us now crackled, but neither of us attempted to move any further. Perhaps it was for the best. We had stayed in that position for a while, looking into each other's eyes, not saying a word, when Brooke's phone rang.

She detangled herself from me and reached for the phone in her pocket; the conversation was brief. I could immediately see her expression fall. "What is it?" I asked, now a bit concerned.

"It's just some work stuff. I got a new assistant, and it looks like she just made a couple of minor screw-ups. I should probably go and deal with it before it becomes an even bigger problem."

"Oh." My voice cracked, unable to hide my disappointment at the absolutely awful timing.

"I've got to go," Brooke said as she got up.

I watched in quiet dismay as Brooke began her exit; an unsettled feeling took

root in my stomach. We had just had a moment, hadn't we? Surely, I couldn't just let
her go. Not without putting up a fight. I
quickly followed behind and found Brooke
standing under a streetlight, trying to hail a
cab. Brooke's eyes caught me as I walked
slowly towards her. The visual under the
light was quite amazing to behold. The soft
light danced beautifully around her hair,
with a radiance that could have had me
staring all night. Brooke watched as I
walked up and stood right in front of her.

"Brooke, wait! Before you go, I have
something to say."

Brooke nodded silently, waiting for me
to say something, but I couldn't. My
mouth was slightly open, trying to say
something, anything, but nothing came to
mind. That's when I decided to act; it was
better than looking like a complete fool in
front of her. Throwing all caution to the
wind, I inclined my head, took Brooke's
cheeks into my hands and kissed her. It
was rash, it was impulsive, but in that moment, it felt bold. It was amazing. Brooke
didn't react immediately, but she didn't
pull away from me either. Before long, her

hands were on my waist as she pulled me into her, deepening the kiss. Brooke and I had kissed before; however, this felt different but no less amazing. It was one of those toe-curling kinds of kisses. The kind that felt like a glass of cold fresh water in the heat of summer. My body buzzed in that special kind of way that only Brooke could elicit. In that moment, my brain took the back seat as my body took over, thrumming in the most wonderful way. When our lips parted, I couldn't help but feel the loss.

"Whoa," Brooke said quietly.

"I know," I responded, similarly tongue-tied.

Minutes later, one of New York's famous yellow cabs pulled up right next to us. "I guess that's my ride," Brooke said, breathing hard, evidently still reeling from the effects of our kiss. Without thinking twice, I tugged on her arm. "Don't go. Come upstairs with me."

My heart was beating wildly as Brooke's eyes scanned mine; the heavy intensity within them completely laid bare. I could see the mental calculations going on in her head; it was obvious she wanted this just as much as I did.

"For another nightcap?" she asked, referencing our first night together, that wry smile on her face.

"This time, it's a glass of wine," I responded, my heart beating wildly. I was suddenly feeling extremely aware of every part of my body.

"Alright," Brooke responded before profusely apologizing to the driver and hailing off the cab. We looked into each other's eyes as the reality of what just happened sunk in.

"Come with me," I said as I led Brooke back to the hotel and into the elevator. As Brooke stood next to me on the elevator, just the warmth from her body elicited a warm feeling that swirled wildly between my legs. I wondered if Brooke felt, too, that all-too-familiar stirring that went from the top of my head all the way to the bottom of my feet. Thankfully the ride was short; immediately, when we got into the room, all bets were off. When I closed the door, I turned around to find Brooke standing directly behind me, the softness that was previously in her eyes now replaced by something much more serious. Brooke was about two inches taller, but as I stood there, my face right next to hers, it felt minimal. Brooke held my gaze as she pulled me in before running her hands up my arms, over my collarbone before cradling my face. My body ached for her desperately. At that moment, Brooke was everything I wanted. All my logical senses had taken their leave, leaving me at the mercy of just how much I ached for Brooke. Brooke brushed her lips against mine, lightly at first, before fully going in for the kiss. Unable to help myself, I pushed myself into her. Her mouth was warm and felt like all kinds of wonderful, unleashing a wildness within me. The heat in my underwear began to grow, expanding wildly with each moment Brooke's lips touched mine.

"I missed this," I said when we finally parted, and I was finally able to gasp for air.

"Me too," Brooke said as she flashed me a reassuring smile before taking hold of my hand and leading me to the bed.

We sat on the bed kissing, our lips entirely out of control, taking on a wild rhythm of their own. Brooke ran her hand up and down my thighs as I did my best to undo the buttons of the shirt that kept me from what it was that I deeply craved. Once the offending article of clothing had been successfully removed, I took my place on Brooke's lap, taking in the beauty of the gorgeous woman underneath me. Without breaking eye contact, I slid my hand down Brooke's cheek, down to her neck before circling her breasts. Without warning, I descended straight for her neck, unleashing a multitude of slow, sensual kisses. Brooke let me willingly, moaning softly into my ear every time I bit gently into her. Her hands covered my breasts fully, circling my nipples slowly. Seemingly tired of the t-shirt that was acting as the impediment to her efforts, Brooke tugged at the hem of my shirt, masterfully pulling it over my head.

"Christ," Brooke breathed in as she took in the visual of me, completely topless on top of her. Slowly she kissed me, starting with my neck and then lower from the top of my breasts, downwards, until without warning, Brooke took me into her. The warmth of her mouth on my nipple as she slowly sucked, her other hand circling my other breast, was nearly enough for me to come undone. Yearning for more, I pushed myself against her, our bodies thrumming with arousal as we settled into an easy rhythm. Deep, sensual moans escaped my lips as I rocked against her, completely taken.

Suddenly Brooke stopped. "I think we are overdressed," she said as she opened the button of my pants and began to slide them down my thighs before ridding me of my now-soaked panties.

"Not fair," I said, referring to the fact that she still had her pants and sports bra on. "Not to worry. I am more than happy to remove them," I said as I quickly got the clothing off of her. For a second, I stood there breathless; the visual of this gorgeous woman fully naked in front of me was something I was never going to get used to. Brooke pulled me into her, and the tantalizing kissing continued as she pushed my back into the mattress and got on top of me.

"Let me make love to you," she said softly, but there was something in her eyes, a desire like none I had ever seen before. I nodded slowly, giving her permission to do as she pleased with me.

Masterfully she settled on top of me, her thigh taking its place in between my legs. My muscles turned to liquid as I rocked against her. I closed my eyes, taking in all the sensations as our motion settled into a slow, sensual rhythm. As the intense aching between my thighs increased, I moaned softly into Brooke's mouth, with every moment becoming more and more desperate for release. Not wanting to let go, I wrapped my legs around her waist. Sensing how close I was, Brooke slipped two fingers inside me and started off slow before adding a finger and then another. Little jolts of pleasure combined to form what felt like a tidal wave with each firm movement from her hand. I felt wide open for her and the sensation of stretching open for her blew me away. I wanted so badly to close my eyes, but I found myself transfixed, unable to take my eyes off Brooke's. She was too beautiful to take my eyes off of, but soon enough, the orgasm that was building slowly, moving steadily from a tingly in my toes, rose quickly, washing over me and sending me to highs that only Brooke could take me to. I arched into her, shaking uncontrollably, gasping for air, unable to utter a single word. As I slowly came down from my orgasm, I lay there, all the raw feelings swirling inside me as Brooke laid next to me, pulling me into her.

"I love you," I blurted out, slight tears in my eyes, unable to control the emotions that were now fully at the surface. Brooke paused and looked at me tenderly, obviously taking in my words. "I love you too, Sloane," she said and stroked my cheek with her thumb. I turned to my side as Brooke placed her arms around me and pulled in to spoon me. Nothing could beat this. At that moment, life and all its worries melted away, and for those few hours, everything felt good with the world.

15

BROOKE

A tiny ray of light seeped in through the corner of the curtain and shone right onto my face, reluctantly pulling me out of the wonderfully relaxing sleep I was in. Still drowsy, I pulled Sloane closer. This was what I had dreamed of every day for the past six months, I didn't know what it meant or if it would work, but I had to at least try and see it through this time. I smiled as Sloane shifted positions and pushed herself into me, lighting my body up in the most wonderful way, and the wonderful memories of the night before came flooding back. We had gone all night, the first time we had fallen asleep, but in her usual way, Sloane hadn't been done with me yet, waking me up to finish what we had started. And God, it was amazing. I had been used to dominating women, but Sloane was just something else. For some reason, giving over my control to her felt right; it always felt right. Slowly, I pulled myself away just enough to reach for my phone on the bedside table. *Oh shit.* It was already 7:15, I had a meeting at 9:00, and I needed to get ready.

I lay there, enjoying the feeling for a few moments before slowly detangling myself from Sloane and beginning the hunt for my clothes on the hotel room floor. Luckily, it was only a few minutes before I was fully dressed and ready to go. I looked at Sloane as she shifted beautifully in her sleep.

"Hey, sleepyhead," I said as I shook her, to which she stirred a little and shifted to the other side. Just as I expected, dead as a doornail. Sloane was a much heavier sleeper than anyone I had ever met in my life; a hurricane probably couldn't wake her if it tried. I would have to leave a note. The window I had to get to my apartment, freshen up, and get to my meeting was already tight enough; delaying any longer would wreak havoc on my schedule for the rest of the day. If I had any chance of attending the match Sloane had invited me to later in the day, I had to get on top of things quickly. It wasn't going to be easy to fix my schedule, but was anything to do with Sloane ever easy? I smiled unwittingly to myself; somehow, I think I preferred it that way. It kept things interesting, even if that pissed me off sometimes.

Quickly I plucked out a page from one of the branded notepads on the counter and wracked my brain, trying my best to think of something quirky or cute. Nothing. Giving up, I was about to write a bland, to-the-point message when I heard her voice from behind me.

"I didn't think it was your style to dine and dash," Sloane's voice called from underneath the covers.

I smiled as I turned my eyes away from the sheet of paper in front of me and on to Sloane. "It isn't. But I do have a meeting I have to get to."

"Fair enough," Sloane managed as she

adjusted herself in bed. "I still have until 10:00 before I have to get out there for a walk and stretch."

"Lucky you. And don't sweat it; you're going to kill it today, Sloane."

"I hope so," came the reply, in that heightened tone that told me that even she didn't believe what she was saying.

I walked over to the bed and sat down. "Hey, look at me," I called out, prompting that sweet face to show up from underneath the covers. "You're going to do great. I know Jane Parker is a big deal for you to start with. Your confidence took a hit, but don't let that bring you down, Sloane. You are the champion. Remember everything you have won in your playing career. None of these players can touch you. You have put so much energy into the recovery and trained harder than anyone I've ever known. You are completely recovered and fitter than you have ever been. You are a great athlete; you are going to kill it today. I believe in you."

Sloane smiled at me. "Thanks, Brooke."

"Anything for my lady," I said as I planted a quick kiss on her lips.

"So, I'm your lady now?" Sloane asked. The playfulness was fully on display in her eyes, but I knew the implications of that question. What I didn't know was if I could ever get used to how fast things changed with this woman.

"How about we save that conversation for tonight? We can talk about it over a nice dinner to celebrate your win."

"Sounds perfect," Sloane said, flashing that beautiful smile in my direction.

I planted another kiss on her before picking up my phone and wallet and heading out for the day. This day had begun even more perfectly than I could have hoped. Everything from the air to my morning coffee was somehow better. I couldn't wipe the grin off my face; I had to admit, having Sloane in my life again did make everything brighter.

16

"You're lucky your little stunt worked out; otherwise, I would have had your head for breakfast," I said to Tiffany as we walked through the entrance of the Louis Armstrong Stadium.

"I know," she said glibly. "But you wouldn't have done anything if not for me. So really, I deserve a dinner in my honor."

I rolled my eyes. "Okay, fine. But don't do anything like that again. It could have blown up in my face."

"But it didn't." Tiffany's expression changed to that usual cheeky disposition. "I bumped into Brooke in the lobby this morning. And from where I was standing, it looked like she was still wearing yesterday's suit, so I know things must have gone well. Very well," she said before flashing me that mischievous smile.

I couldn't help but smile as the red hit my cheeks. "Oh, you have no idea."

"This way, Miss Smith," the usher who had just joined us directed as he led us into a hallway. We had just arrived at the intersection of the hallway when the usher alerted us that was the farthest Tiffany could come with me as the rest of the section was reserved for players only.

"Good Luck, Smith," Tiffany said as she kissed my cheek before heading off to have a snack at one of the concessions stands and later taking her place in the stands.

I quickly took the elevator to the locker room and got changed. Without delay, I grabbed my racket and got out onto the practice court. I had no intention of meeting Jane in the locker room and participating in any petty psychological battles. I had come here to win, and to do that I needed to be in the best mental state. I did a few stretches by myself; I loved to be alone before any kind of competition. I didn't need any form of distraction to prevent me from gaining the momentum I needed.

"You're up next, Miss Smith," one of the ushers alerted me. *You've got this,* I said over and over as I followed him through the corridor under the stands and bypassed him as I got into the arena. Walking to take my place on my end of the court, I noticed Brooke walking to her seat in the front row right next to Tiffany. Those two were quickly becoming friends. The assurance of Brooke's place sent a settling feeling of calmness that washed over me, relaxing my nerves and did wonders to boost my confidence.

After quieting the crowd, the match kicked off. Since I had won the coin toss, I had the opportunity to serve first. I bounced the ball repeatedly to the ground before grabbing it, throwing it in the air, and smacking it hard with my racket across the court, sending it hurling to Jane's side of the court. The shot was so fast she faltered; her response was a second too slow, missing the ball. I threw my fist in the air in quick celebration as a surge of confidence took over.

Excellent   start,   Sloane,   I   thought, bouncing the ball to the ground once more before raising it in the air and hitting it across to my opponent's side, spinning. Jane sprung to receive the ball, just narrowly catching and hitting it with both her hands on the racket. The ball zoomed quickly towards my side before hitting the net and slowing down. It was an easy target. Stretching my arms out, I managed to hit it hard enough to land on Jane's side just after crossing the net. But she was too far to receive the ball, and by the time she caught up with it, it had already bounced twice. This was turning out better than I expected. I knew I had trained hard for this, but Jane Parker must have done me the favor of underestimating me; this was seeming a little too easy.

The match continued as Jane picked up speed. I might have spoken too soon as she picked up the pace and caught me, taking a set for herself. I gripped the ball as one of the ball boys handed it to me. This was it; I had pushed her to match point. My serve.

Nervously I shuffled by the baseline, bouncing the ball, trying to get a hold of my emotions. This was nerve-wracking; the game had been brutal, but if I didn't win this one, I was almost certainly going to be forgotten in the trashcan of the has-beens of tennis. I was starting to lose focus; this wasn't good. I turned my attention to the audience to find Brook smiling at me. That comforting smile always made me remember just how much I was capable of. "You can do this, Sloane," I muttered to myself. "You can do this, you are a champion. You are one of the greats." I said as I threw the ball into the air and whacked it as hard as I could. After a series of back-and-forth shots, I hit the ball once more, sending it to the far right of the court, too far for her reach. The game was complete. Just like that, I had won. It was unbelievable; a surge of emotion coursed through me. I was nothing less than ecstatic. I walked over to the net and shook hands with Jane.

"Congratulations, Smith. That was a great comeback."

I simply nodded, unsure of what to do next. This was only a first round match but due to Jane's top seeding and me being an ex champion, the audience was packed and the journalists were lurking. That's when it hit me. This was my chance to finally make a statement. In a move that was totally uncharacteristic, adrenaline pumping, I jogged over to the barricade that separated the court from the stands. Gracefully, I stretched over to Brooke, took her face into my hands, and kissed her passionately as Tiff and the people seated next to her broke into a round of applause and cameras began to snap. The feel of Brooke's lips in that adrenaline-pumped moment was way more than I had bargained for. It felt intense and overwhelming in the most wonderful way. This was it; this was everything I had ever wanted, right in front of me. I leaned my forehead against Brooke and smiled as I breathed in hard. In all the excitement, I had forgotten how to breathe. Brooke smiled as I held the sides of her face.

"Sloane, Sloane, is this your girlfriend?" I heard a call and a camera and microphone were thrust into my face.

"Yes, yes she is." I said smiling widely, feeling happier than I had ever felt.

"Are you okay?" Brooke whispered, smiling too as I began to calm down.

"I've never been better."

EPILOGUE

BROOKE

The view of the city from our new penthouse in Tribeca was nothing less than breathtaking. I stood perfectly in awe at the views of the sun setting just over the city skyline. The spectacular reds and ambers radiated from the fiery orb melded together perfectly against the blue background as if brushed upon a canvas by the most magnificent of artists.

"Those new sponsors of yours aren't going to be happy if we get there late," I called out from the balcony. Sloane was taking longer than usual to get ready. I guess it was understandable; this was her first dinner with the executives from

Sportek, the up-and-coming sports equipment company known for their draw to athletes with an authentic and bold public image to be the face of their brand. The kiss between Sloane and me at her US Open first round match had been enough to catch their eye, but her spectacular performance for those brutal two weeks and her taking the trophy was more than enough for them to make her the official face of the brand. But it wasn't just their attention we had caught; companies had come in, falling over themselves trying to have some sort of partnership with Sloane. It was amazing to watch. Sloane Smith was back. She had won another slam and confidently so, she had come out publicly, she was every inch the champion she used to be and she was more popular than ever.

"We can go now," she called out.

My mouth dropped as she appeared in the doorway in a sexy strapless burgundy dress and black heels. Her beautiful thick honey hair descended into exquisite waves down past her shoulders. The diamond earrings that dangled oh so slightly in her ears shone in the reflection of the sunset behind me. I stood there speechless; this woman was nothing less than a work of art.

"Come on. Let's get going; we don't have all night," she said, a tiny smile tugging at the corner of her lips. She knew exactly what kind of reaction she was going to get from me in that dress.

"If you were any more gorgeous, my heart would stop. I wouldn't be able to handle it," I said as I took a step closer to Sloane and inclined my head for a kiss. The kiss was deep, slow, the perfect dance to start the evening with.

"Wow. I am never going to get used to that," she said. Those deep eyes looked at me, cutting their way into my soul.

"I know." The incredible sensation of kissing Sloane somehow always felt new.

"Let's get going. Any more of this, and we might find ourselves ditching the whole thing and staying indoors to do more of *that*," she said, shooting me a naughty look that almost had me considering the idea.

"Alright," I said, suppressing a grin. Sloane had the uncanny ability to say exactly what I was thinking.

We got into the car downstairs and

headed straight to the venue for the dinner. The past two months had been nothing less than spectacular. Save for one or two negative articles, the response to Sloane's coming out had been overwhelmingly positive. Honestly, it had more than superseded all our expectations. Sloane still had a long way to go getting used to all the attention our personal lives were getting, but watching her handle everything before things eventually settled down was a celebration all on its own. She had made it perfectly clear to the world that she was done with hiding who she was and who she loved. It had been a long time coming, but she had never seemed freer, and I had never felt more special or cared for. She was in incredible physical shape, playing some of her best tennis and was climbing back up the world rankings. She honestly looked unbeatable lately.

Thankfully the drive to the Luxe Hotel was short; the event was already in full swing as we arrived.

"And if it isn't the woman of the hour." Coach Dan smiled as he approached us.

"How is it looking, Coach? Cause it

seems like you've got all these fancy executives eating right out of your hands," Sloane teased the man.

"They want to put your face on everything now, you are the player of the moment," he responded, sipping on a glass of champagne.

"Look who's becoming a superstar," I chimed in.

Coach smiled at Sloane and then turned his attention back to me. "We wouldn't be here if not for you. Thanks a lot, Brooke. I really mean that."

"Anything for her," I said, glancing at Sloane as I rubbed the small of her back.

Just as Dan was talking to Sloane about their next match, a stout gentleman who I later realized was Sloane's new publicist, walked towards us. "If you two looked any more in love, I would have to fling my lonely heart out that window."

"Well, Jim, if you didn't spend all your time at these events schmoozing with these old executives, maybe you would have met your very own Brooke," Sloane replied jokingly as she tugged at my arm.

"That would have hurt if you hadn't just

made me so much money," Jim replied slyly before setting his eyes on another person he needed to go speak to. "I've seen the finished ad. You're going to love it," he said before briskly walking in the direction of the stage.

We were chatting with Dan when the live band switched to "Your song" by Elton John. It was one of our favorite songs.

"May I have this dance?" Sloane asked, her eyes on mine, a slow-burning intensity in them.

"Definitely," I said as she excused us before taking hold of my hand and leading me to the dance floor.

As my left arm encircled her, Sloane took hold of my right as we began our slow glide.

"I could never have done all this without you," she said as she leaned her head over my shoulder.

"All I need is just a kiss and some chocolate, and we can consider your debt paid," I said as I smiled down at her.

"Might be a little tricky, but I'll see what I can do," Sloane responded as we each took a step in time with the music.

"You could start with the first instalment right now," I said, raising a suggestive eyebrow.

Sloane chuckled knowingly before taking hold of my face with her hands and planting a kiss that sent a wave of warmth to every part of my body. As if right on cue, the head of advertising from Sportek took hold of the mic, welcoming the guests, who slowly began to quiet down. After giving the background of the company's desire to always be first and support authenticity, he applauded Sloane for being brave and going against the grain by refusing to be held down by societal expectations. Sloane held onto my hand with one hand as she waved at the crowd that had already burst into applause with the other. It felt so surreal that all this could be accomplished simply by choosing to live as the authentic version of ourselves.

The large screen at the front of the room flickered as the campaign for Sportek's new range of tennis equipment capably modeled by Sloane alongside the booming voice of a narrator and edgy theme music flashed across the screen. The commercial was short and captivating as the moving images and music brought everything to life in the most energetic way.

I couldn't help but smile as the thunderous applause from the crowd took over, indicating the campaign's launch.

"To us," I said, raising a glass to Sloane as the attention finally faded away from us. Sloane's glass met mine before we each finished our drinks.

Sloane took a step close and pulled me in. "I think I'm beat. I would like to go home now and deliver on the second instalment of my promise."

"The guest of honor leaving her own party? How scandalous!" I said as I grinned down at her.

"Unfortunately, only our bedroom can accommodate the kind of things I plan to do tonight," she said without taking her eyes off mine.

"It would be my pleasure to take you," I blushed a little, knowing precisely what she was implying.

We said a few quick goodbyes before heading out into the car that had brought us.

Sloane and I sat quietly holding hands in the back of the car as we headed home. *Home.* The word struck me. I had spent my whole life moving around, searching for a home, and it had cost me dearly. But as I looked down at Sloane, I realized that home for me wasn't a place. Whether we were in Miami or New York, or even all the way across the world, I would always be home because Sloane had turned out to be that for me.

"I love you," Sloane spoke as she looked up at me, breaking the comfortable silence that had taken over the ride.

"I love you too," I replied, knowing just how deeply the sentiment meant for me. Sloane and I were headed home. To our apartment and our life, and as she sat there, her eyes squarely on mine, there was nothing more I could ask for.

The End

BONUS SCENE

Thank you so much for buying and reading my book!

As usual, there is a FREE erotic bonus scene to accompany this book for my VIP readers. If you are on my mailing list it will be sent out to you automatically via e-mail on Monday 17th May 2021 the day after the release of the book.

If you aren't on my mailing list and would like to become a VIP reader to access this scene and all future free erotic bonus scenes then please go to the following link: https://BookHip.com/QXGFQPJ where you can download the bonus scene, Strawberries and Cream. If you struggle with the link, please do email me at emilyhayeswrites@hotmail.com and I will email you a copy.

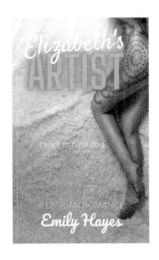

Can you make love work with someone from an entirely different world? Elizabeth Diamond runs an exclusive art gallery. It would be highly unprofessional of her to get involved with a wild young artist in this Rich Girl/Poor Girl Age Gap romance. getbook.at/Art

Can single mom, Megan's charms melt the frozen heart of her Ice Queen boss in this hot age gap office romance?

http://getbook.at/Headmistress

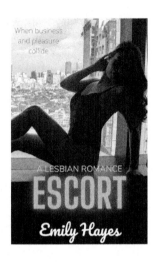

When business and pleasure collide

A LESBIAN ROMANCE

ESCORT

Emily Hayes

Wealthy business woman, Ashley Davidson hires an escort to pretend to be her girlfriend. When the chemistry between them heats up, will they keep things strictly business in this sexy Butch-Femme Romance?

http://getbook.at/EHEscort

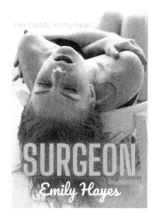

A FOREST VALE MEDICAL ROMANCE

Her hands on my heart...

SURGEON

Emily Hayes

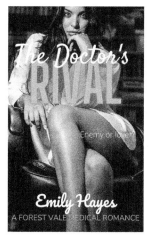

The Doctor's

RIVAL

Enemy or lover?

Emily Hayes

A FOREST VALE MEDICAL ROMANCE

Forest Vale Medical Romance Series:

Book 1: World class heart Surgeon Katherine Ross meets a mysterious young woman on a dating app and their chemistry together is incredible. When their true identities are revealed what will they do in this hot age gap romance?

http://getbook.at/Surgeon

Book 2: Ex Army Doctor Hollis Roman is always right. She doesn't expect to be challenged by anyone on her medical expertise, far less by a feisty paramedic. A very attractive feisty paramedic. Can they keep things professional in this Enemies to Lovers butch-femme romance?

http://getbook.at/TDR

Book 3: Hardworking Nurse, Eve Foster, can't stop thinking about the beautiful medical receptionist. But the hot older woman is straight, isn't she?

A hot Age Gap Medical Christmas Romance

getbook.at/XmasEve

Book 4: Doctor Lillian Foster is head of Obstetrics. She is career focussed and never distracted. Her new patient is sexy as hell and flirting like crazy with her. Can she resist?

A hot Age Gap Doctor-Patient Romance

getbook.at/SMP

Hers Box Set

Follow Lauren as she explores her desires at the exclusive women only club Lix. The owner of the club is the handsome, yet guarded Quinn and Lauren is attracted to her immediately. Can she find a way to break down Quinn's walls and explore all of her own fantasies in this Age Gap Butch-Femme erotic romance.

getbook.at/Hers

Printed in Great Britain
by Amazon